ACCLAIM FOR

THE POLITICS OF CHRISTMAS

"*Sweet Home Alabama* meets *The Family Stone* in this incredibly fun and candy-cane-sweet holiday romcom. An adorable and satisfying page turner that will fill you up with all the Hallmark Christmas feels this holiday season!" — Chelsea Bobulski, author of the *All I Want for Christmas* series

"*The Politics of Christmas* is more than just a sweet, Christmas story. Miss Taylor uses witty banter and faith messages to weave a beautiful story of second chances and forgiveness. It's a story that makes you reflect on your own life choices and how they affect those around you, while also providing the reader with hope that God can use all the broken pieces of our lives to create something beautiful." — Latisha Sexton, author of *Single Dad Center* and *Bram Baxter Marries the Wrong Sister*

"In *The Politics of Christmas*, author Drew Taylor explores themes of family, faith, and forgiveness with brave insights and a tender resolution. Her second-chance romance is a must-read for anyone who appreciates self-reflection and sacrifice in the pursuit of lasting love." — Julie Christianson, author of *Apple Valley* and *Abieville Love Stories*

"*The Politics of Christmas* is a fun Christmas read that can be enjoyed any time of the year! The story contains a strong thread of faith that weaves authentically and flawlessly through the pages. There was a perfect balance between deep themes and humorous banter. I thoroughly enjoyed this book and would recommend it to anyone in search of a fun, faith-filled, Christmas read!" — Tawni Suchy, author of the *Forever Duet* series

THE POLITICS
OF
Christmas

A SECOND CHANCE ROM-COM BY
DREW TAYLOR

Cover Design by Drew Taylor

Character/Tree Art by Callie McLay

Developmental Edits by Anne J. Hill

Proofread by Lindsay Rankin

www.drewtaylorwrites.com

DEDICATION

To Jesus Christ, my Lord and Savior.

You get all my firsts—including this book.

PROLOGUE

Stella, Ten Years Ago

I quickly dab the sweat beads from the top of my cheeks and forehead as Lucas approaches on his hunter-green four-wheeler. I've been sitting on the front porch for only five minutes, but the Mississippi heat in July is too hot to bear. Tucking my compact and cloth back into my little brown backpack, I throw a gleaming smile his way as he rides up beside me.

"Stell Bells." Lucas waves, using the nickname he gave me in eighth grade. I love bells, especially Christmas bells. The sounds of bells are beautiful, and Lucas thought I was the most beautiful thing on the east side of the Mississippi River. Or so he told me after I pestered him to explain the real reason behind the nickname at our high school graduation party last month.

I pick up two dripping glasses of sweet tea, handing him mine as a joke. After eyeing the pink lip gloss stain on the side, he takes my cup.

"Luca." I laugh, using his own nickname, pulling back my glass. "I've already drunk out of this one."

"And that's why I want it." He smiles the crooked smile that makes me weak in my knees. Hopping down from the ATV, he takes my glass and drinks a big swig. After setting the cup down on the four-wheeler, he sweeps me into his arms, kissing me like there was no tomorrow. *Oh, how I'll miss his sweet kisses, tasting of sunshine, mint, and sweet tea.* Breaking free, Lucas jumps on the four-wheeler and pats the back seat.

"Where are we going?" I ask, recalling the text earlier that simply read: *Be ready in thirty minutes.*

"To the house." His words are drowned out by the roar of the ATV. I wrap my arms around his waist, soaking in every moment. In a few short weeks, we will be going to different colleges. Though Mississippi College and Juniper Grove University are only an hour and a half apart, it won't be the same as living five minutes away from each other.

We arrive at the farm shed on his family's tea farm. He jumps off the four-wheeler and offers a hand to me. I take it, mostly because I love the feel of his hand in mine—rough callouses on satin smooth skin. Without letting go, he leads me inside the shed. Lucas opens the doors and I let out a gasp, my free hand flying over my mouth.

The shed has been transformed. All the equipment needed to run the farm has been relocated and a table stands in the middle of the floor with pictures of us—from when we were in diapers to now. Lights are strung across the ceiling, giving the room a romantic, tinted glow. Another table sits in the back of the room filled with desserts, fruit with whipped dip, and sweet tea. With my free hand still covering my open mouth, I turn to meet Lucas's warm caramel eyes. My stomach twists and turns.

With a shy smile, Lucas pulls my hand from my face and slides down onto one knee, never breaking eye contact with me. *No, no, no...*

Time stands still. I should want this. I do want this. Lucas Grady is the love of my life. How lucky am I to have grown up with the man who complements me in every way?

So why am I about to vomit?

"Stella, I have loved you since I discovered girls didn't, in fact, have cooties in middle school. Every time I pulled your hair or teased you in elementary school, it was because I loved you and didn't know how else to show it. I knew I wanted a real relationship with you in eighth grade—from the moment you didn't laugh when I tripped over the soccer ball but reached down to help me up, dusting the grass and dirt from my shirt. By the grace of God, you said yes when I asked you to that last middle school dance. We are fixing to go to college, and I couldn't start this new phase of life without asking you an important question: You're beautiful, and I love you with what little I have. And I will love you until my last dying breath. Will you give me the absolute privilege of becoming my wife?" I think he is holding a ring, but my head is spinning, and the world is blurring.

My chest continually tightens, my heart beating way too fast.

Air. I need air.

With a look that I pray portrays "I'm so very sorry," I dash out of the room that is closing in on me.

I run.

I run through the rows of tea leaves and into the woods. I run until I reach the treehouse Lucas and I played in as kids. The one we snuck into only a week ago for a midnight picnic. Before I know it, I find myself sitting on the floor of the treehouse with my knees glued to my chest while I rock back and forth.

I'm eighteen. I can't get married.

But I love him. He is the one for me. We fit.

Dad is supposed to be here.

The battle rages in my mind like I'm back on the debate team, though this time it's me versus me.

A body leans against mine, arms wrapping me up from behind. His scent envelops me—sunshine, mint, and fresh earth.

A feeling of safety floods over me as Lucas sits behind me, holding me like he's never letting go.

In, out.

My breathing slows as a throbbing pulse settles in my head. The way it does after every panic attack.

"Thank you," I whisper, letting my head fall against his chest and my legs splay out. I place my arms on top of his as he continues to hold me. And it hits me—Lucas is my safe place. No matter what, no matter the distance between us... We will and can make it.

"Yes," I breathe. I feel him stiffen behind me. Finagling my way out of his hold, I turn to face him, resting on my knees...

"Stella, hold on–" Lucas begins, but I interrupt him, taking his hands in mine.

"Yes, Lucas. I'll marry you. We have a lot to work out with college and all, but it's only an hour and a half away from each other. We can be engaged, even if we have to wait four years to walk the aisle."

"Then what was all that?" His eyebrows furrow as he tilts his head slightly to the side.

"Shock. Surprise." I throw words out. *You're eighteen*, a voice inside my head reiterates. I tell it to go fall in a hole. "Dad was supposed to be here."

"You know, Stella, before he died, he told me that one day he would give me his blessing." Tears begin to gather in my eyes. "I didn't know what that meant, since I was only fifteen at the time. But the words stuck, and I understand now."

"He gave you his blessing…" My world shifts again, this time for the better. It's like Dad is affirming this from heaven.

Lucas nods his head.

"Let's do this," I say with new determination. If Dad saw it—if he wanted it—then I know it's right.

"Okay," he says softly, breathing like all is settled in the world.

I give him a smile in return. "Okay."

With that, he slips a silver band that hosts a small, marquise-cut diamond onto my ring finger.

A perfect fit.

After spending the rest of the afternoon with our families and friends, he drops me off at my house. Mama, who had left the party early, sits on the front porch swing.

"How was the rest of your night, sweetie?" she asks as I sit down next to her.

"Like riding the Tilt-a-Whirl." I laugh. "But in the best way."

"So, you're doing this?" I look over Mama's face. Crow's feet sit on the edges of her eyes, marking her years of laughter, shenanigans, and spirit. I grab her hands, feeling the swollen joints in her palms and fingers.

"Yes, Mama. I'm doing this."

"I guess I can throw this away then?" She removes her hands from mine and reaches to grab an envelope—more like a folder—off the table beside the swing. She hands it to me, and every decision I've made tonight goes up in flames.

"It's from Harvard University..." I say, tracing the name on the folder. The *thick* folder.

"Open it." Mama nudges me with her elbow.

Without further hesitation, I rip the package open. Pulling the contents out, I read the note sitting in front of a booklet that reads "Welcome to Harvard".

"Dear Stella Harper." I pause to wipe away the moisture building in my eyes. "Congratulations! We are pleased to inform you that the Committee of Admissions and Financial Aid has offered you a position in the graduating Class of..." I stop reading, meet Mama's steel-gray eyes, and burst out in something between a laugh and a cry.

"You got in, baby! I knew you could do it!" Mama stands slowly, and I jump to meet her in a hug.

"I got into Harvard!" I screech in a voice that could wake the slumbering wildlife around me. I'd been waitlisted, and I thought for sure I wasn't going to get in. Especially this late in the summer. Classes will start in only a few weeks. Unwrapping my hands from around Mama, I catch a glimmer of a diamond ring on my finger.

I got into Harvard...a thousand plus whatever miles away from Dasher Valley, Mississippi.

From home.

From Lucas Grady.

"**A**re you going?" Lucas's voice is like barbed wire, tangling around me and cutting me in every direction. I thought he would be happy for me.

"This is everything I've ever wanted," I plead. He knows this. He knows!

"Even above marrying me?"

"How can you say that Lucas? How dare you!" I can't stop the flood of lava spewing from my mouth. "I love you with every fiber of my being. You are my best friend, my fiancé! For heaven's sake, I said yes!"

"Before something better came along," he scoffs, the words striking like a venomous snake sinking its fangs into my skin.

"I'm here to make this work! We can do long distance." My heart shudders. "Marriage is about supporting one another, right? I want to do soul-changing work through politics. I want this!"

How can a healthy marriage begin when he wants to hold me back from something I want so badly?

"It's just a silly dream, Stella. What can a girl from Small Town, Mississippi, hope to ever change in this huge world?" My breath hitches, and I stand there looking into the brown eyes I once thought bore the very sun in them. Now, they look as dead as the leaves in autumn. His words are like a disease that consumes the mind. They have latched onto me, and I fear they won't let go.

"We'll talk about this later. I need to think." Lucas shakes his head before turning on his heel and barging back into his home. I stand there, twisting the ring still encircling my finger, watching the door close on everything I thought I wanted.

My chest constricts and I climb into my car with shaky hands and labored breaths. *God, let me make it home before this panic attack completely takes over.*

ONE

STELLA

T his is THE day. The day I have been dreaming of ever since
Mama told me my ideas could change the world. After successfully getting the new governor of New York elected a few weeks
ago, I put myself on a political hiatus until after the new year to take
a break from the news cycle. Even the best of us find ourselves in
a deep depression hole after a while. That is until a certain young
hotshot, attractive billionaire called me up two weeks ago asking
me to do the one thing I've wanted to do since I was just a girl.

Stella Harper—Presidential Campaign Manager.

"Where is Darcy Marshall?" the head of the directing team at
Buzz News asks me. Sweat pricks at my forehead, but I force my
face to remain smooth as stone. *Be cool, Stella. You haven't lost
the billionaire.* Where did he run off to? "He goes on in five," the
exasperated man continues. I open my mouth to state that he will
be here shortly when a familiar gruff voice speaks from behind me.

"I'm right here." I breathe a sigh of relief at the sound of Mr. Marshall's voice. Not that he has ever been late, but this is definitely NOT the day to be late. "Where do I need to be?"

The directing team sweeps Mr. Marshall off to sit next to Diane Parvin on the set of America's News Hive. I send a quick text to Micah, the social media coordinator of our campaign, to make sure he is posting about Mr. Marshall going live on Buzz in—I check my smartwatch—three minutes.

"Breathe," Hayden Bennett, my best friend and assistant manager, whispers as she saunters past me to give Mr. Marshall his notes. He dismisses her, saying he doesn't need notes while tapping his temple with a wink. Hayden whips around, her back to Mr. Marshall. She wears an expression that could make Scrooge himself cower in fear as she advances toward me.

"Arrogant man," she hisses, fiddling with a tightly wound black curl that has come loose from her top bun.

"Hayden, we *want* him to know his talking points without notes. It portrays astuteness and shows he is a polished man." I raise an eyebrow, questioning her flustered state. Hayden and Mr. Marshall must have been natural-born enemies or something. From the moment they met, it was instant dislike. Loathing, really.

"He would do well to be more...likable," she says, tucking her curl back into her bun.

"He's a billionaire." I snort in the most unladylike way. After glancing around to make sure no one heard that, I continue, "His money makes him likable."

Hayden and I stand to the side, watching the directors count down to the show resuming from the commercial break.

Diane Parvin begins, announcing her guest tech billionaire, inventor of the new hot networking app COFFEE, and CEO of Marshall Enterprise—Darcy Marshall.

I clutch my binder to my chest and push my reading glasses down from my nose. This is THE moment.

"Darcy, rumors have been circulating that you have quite the announcement?" Parvin asks, tilting her head to the side. "Ready to let the world in on that secret of yours?"

With a light-hearted chuckle and a nod, he responds. "In fact, I am. Diane, I am happy to announce my bid for the presidency on the Independent Party ticket."

"The Independent Party?" She leans in. "Do you have any fears of not winning due to the sheer seismic power of the two main parties?"

"No fear at all, Diane. I'll tell you why in one name—Stella Harper." Parvin's eyes grow wide as Mr. Marshall nods his head in clear approval, his dirty blonde hair not staying in its slicked-back position. My heart leaps and flutters, and it takes everything in me to not start my little happy dance—a montage of early 2000s dance moves—in the newsroom studio.

"Stella Harper is managing your campaign?" Diane already knew that, of course. I spoke with her when we arrived. I've got to say, the news anchor knows how to perform.

"Indeed she is." Mr. Marshall steeples his hands and turns directly to the camera, his Pacific Ocean blue eyes penetrating. "I am lucky to have her on my team, and I know together we will see a victory. A victory for the great United States of America!"

"Best of luck to you, Darcy Marshall. And to Stella Harper. I'd say you have a strong shot with that firecracker running your campaign. Her seven years of successfully getting her candidates elected speaks volumes."

"That I do, Diane. I believe we will win." Win we will.

While the interview continues with Diane asking about Mr. Marshall's platform points, why he decided to run, and his plans, my brain is on repeat like the news cycle itself.

I am managing a presidential campaign. Presidential. Campaign.

Merry Christmas to me!

"You are a powerhouse, Stells!" Hayden throws a light brown arm around my shoulders as she whisper-shouts, "You are getting everything you have worked for and dreamed about! You are officially the youngest woman to manage a presidential campaign."

"I know," I squeal like Monica from *Friends*. My body is vibrating like the Energizer Bunny, and I refrain from jumping up and down in my stilettos. Mostly because I WILL break my ankle.

"What's next?" Hayden poses as we watch, her head cocked to the side as her dark eyes remain cemented on Mr. Marshall.

"Diplomatic position overseas?" We both burst out with laughter and earn ourselves several dirty looks. Just...no. That requires a foreign language, which is something I dodged like the plague in college. "I'm not sure," I say with an edge of seriousness coming back. I used to have my life planned out. Then my plans changed on a whim. I set new goals that I've conquered. Now here I am getting a shot at the biggest goal I set for myself.

What *is* next?

Is this still what I want? Or is it time for a new direction?

"No biggie. Let's just make it through this campaign with *Mr. Darcy*," she says his name with a hint of disgust while waggling her eyebrows. It's been a running joke of ours to compare the unsuspecting guy with Hayden's favorite Austenian hero. The funny thing is that he's kind of grumpy when not stationed in front of a camera. Especially with Hayden.

"Let's get him elected as president."

Hayden and I spend the rest of the day consuming excessive amounts of hot cocoa and coffee in the office, planning campaign stops, and narrowing down Mr. Marshall's specific talking points for all the controversial topics of today's society. I contact the social media coordinators and graphic designers on my team and ask them to start dreaming up ways to plaster his gorgeous face on every pamphlet, social media platform, and billboard.

Did I mention how attractive Darcy Marshall is? Not that I am interested. I am fully committed to my career. We are thriving and happy right now, thank you very much. But I will work Mr. Marshall's barely-legal-to-run-for-executive-office age and good looks to my advantage so hard that all the girls who just turned eighteen will run to the polls for him on Election Day next year, regardless of the fact he is not a Republican or a Democrat. Or his unavailable status since he is engaged to the daughter of a wealthy and prominent politician.

To finish the last tasks of the day, I get on the phone with the website design team to offer tweaks to the webpage. Finally, I call the speech team to discuss the main talking points for the campaign. So much to do with so little time. The future of my career depends on this. Wherever it is headed next.

With my checklist done for the day, I sit with my feet propped up on the mahogany coffee table in my small uptown New York apartment playing *Zelda: Breath of the Wild* (my guilty pleasure) while sipping on a glass of well-deserved red wine. I am Level 100 cozy wearing my *ELF* onesie and sitting by the electric fireplace. If only I could waltz into the office wearing this bad boy. Women wearing onesies would take over the world! No matter, I will be successful. Even if it's in a pencil skirt, blouse, jacket, and heels because I am THE Stella Harper—the most sought-after campaign manager in the market for the past three years. *Well, I showed them,* I think to myself with a snicker and a sip of wine.

I recall several obnoxious boys from high school who ardently and persistently let me know that women did not have what it takes to be a snake in the political campaign world. My chest constricts as I think of the one person who told me it was "just a silly dream" and that I was "just a girl from Mississippi." Little did they know that I have gumption and never back down from a challenge—spoken or unspoken. I vowed to myself that I would manage a presidential campaign for a person who would make this country a better place one day. And we would win.

I would shatter glass ceilings. I would be an example for my future daughter and millions of other little girls out there who chose the career-woman lifestyle. Who chose to step into a man's world and play with the snakes.

The ring of my cell phone snaps me back to my successful reality.

"Thing 2" is flashing across my screen for a FaceTime call. I pause my game and pick up my phone.

"Well, well, well. If it isn't the big linebacker himself." My brother, Stone, a football player for Juniper Grove University, laughs on the other end of the line. I soak in his carefree laugh, and my heart sinks with how much I miss him.

"You saw my last game?" he asks, his crystal eyes widening. It's unfair that I got stuck with dull, gray eyes while he got those baby blues.

"Of course. I saw you deliver that lethal sack to Mississippi College's quarterback," I say, taking another sip of wine. "You are crushing it this year. I can't believe you are already a senior!" Joy radiates through his face. I continue, "You never give up on that field. That is what makes you a Harper." He physically swells with pride through the phone screen, and I suddenly remember how crappy a sister I am. I toss my head back with a grunt, mumbling, "I meant to text you after that game. I know it's been a while."

"That's okay." He shrugs. "I'm just glad to know you're watching!" Such a forgiving human being. "Anyway, are you coming home for Christmas this year?"

"I don't think so, buddy. I've got a lot of networking to do." His eyes narrow, both brows wrinkling. I continue, "I've been chosen to run Darcy Marshall's presidential campaign."

"Whoa, that's huge!" His volume escalates. "A couple of people were talking about his app in my Business Capstone class. You've *got* to introduce me at some point. I'll fly up or we can FaceTime."

I chuckle at his ramblings. "Have you told Mom?"

"I'm sure she's seen the news by now." However, I haven't received a text or call from her all day.

"But still. She'd want to hear it from you *personally*," he says. I guess I'm a crappy daughter, too. I should have thought about telling her personally the moment I found out.

"You're right." I tug at the neck of my onesie. "I'll call her when we hang up."

"Oh yeah," he remembers. "So why I called... Mom isn't doing well." My insides grow tight.

"Rheumatoid?"

"Yep. And diabetes. I saw her when I went home last weekend. She needs help." He pops the "p" on the word, something he learned from me, with a shake of his head. I respond with a lengthy sigh. Of course, she does. But the stubborn woman refuses any type of assistance. Marian Harper is the definition of Miss Independent.

Like mother like daughter.

"Look Stells. I'm in college," Stone continues. "I can't take care of her from the JGU campus."

"Have we tried getting her into an assisted living home?" I ask. "Maybe Heritage Assisted Living?"

"'Course I've tried," he says, his eyes shifting downward. "I really wish Dad was still here. I don't know how to handle all this." I want to wrap him in a hug through the phone.

"Me too, buddy." The silence stretches for a few moments. I *just* got the job—the job I've put my blood, sweat, and tears into to earn. Sure, I can leave and work from home. I've known most of the people on my team for years now since we run in the same circles. But I don't want to jeopardize this chance. Mama wouldn't want me to jeopardize it either.

"I've tried to be the man of the family since he died," Stone sniffles. His crystal blue eyes glisten with tears. "It just gets so hard sometimes." Seeing my little brother tear up decides for me.

"Maybe I can come home for a week or two for Christmas. See if I can get her moved into Heritage."

"Stells, that would be amazing." His eyes flick back to me, crinkling in the corners. "And I'll be home for a few days around Christmas. We can have Christmas morning like a family again!" My heart melts like cream cheese on cinnamon rolls at his utter excitement. The kid goes through life looking toward the next bright thing.

"Okay," I breathe. "There is a lot I have to do to make this work, but... I'll see you soon. At home." I can't believe I'm saying those words. I've avoided home the way politicians avoid telling the truth. When I left ten years ago, I had no return date. I was hurt at first. Then after a few years, I was embarrassed at the way I left. Time flew away from me quicker than a hummingbird. Too much time had passed to try and make amends by the time I realized I should.

"Dasher Valley has missed you." He flips his shaggy hair, reminding me of the thirteen-year-old boy I left at home.

"I can't say I've missed it." I laugh, though my insides twist tighter than a Twizzler. "But it will be nice to be in my old stomping grounds for Christmas."

"Dasher Valley does Christmas right." Stone grins, shaking his golden hair from his eyes again.

"Yes, it does." A montage of memories from past Christmases assaults me. There is one thing, or one person, I should say, that made Christmas magical in Dasher Valley. My stomach churns. I'm not ready to face that ghost.

"Stone," a high-pitched feminine voice whines on his end of the phone. "I'm ready to go."

I raise an eyebrow at Stone, who just shrugs with a boyish grin.

"Is this girl number three this week?" I question.

"You'll never know." He winks with a sly grin playing across his face. "See you soon, Seester!" He disconnects, using the version of "sister" that stuck with him as a child.

"See you soon," I whisper to a black screen. *I'm going to Mississippi this Christmas,* I think to myself while wave after wave of nausea threatens the wine sloshing in my stomach to make a reappearance. I send a silent prayer to Jesus that *he* is out of town for Christmas. He still lives in Dasher Valley because the stubborn man would never leave Small Town, Mississippi, but please, *please* let him be away for the holidays. *I'm not ready.*

After calling Mama to tell her the good news about the campaign, I book a quite expensive flight home for Friday the 13th (this is starting well) with a return date for the 27th. A little over two weeks. I can do two weeks.

Right?

TWO

Lucas

He wants me to do *what?!*

Stone Harper is out of his ever-loving mind if he thinks for one second I'm going to drive two and half hours to the Jackson Airport to pick up his sister—the one who left me ten years ago without so much as a note. I make sure I tell him that, too.

"Lucas, please." Stone's blue eyes grow wide. I don't budge, and he sighs. "Look. I know you hate her and all that. I would, too, if I were in your shoes. But I have practice tomorrow and can't get off to pick her up. And you know Mom can't." Curse it all.

"That's low. Using your mother," I grumble. "But what about Gracie? They still talk. Can't she pick her up?"

"I've already asked her, but she can't get away from Honey's. Trust me, you were my last resort."

"Fine," I spit. "You owe me though. Big time."

"You stew on that. I'll send you her flight information." Stone's mischievous grin doesn't go amiss. I can't help but wonder if I was truly his last resort.

I hang up the FaceTime call, throwing my cracked iPhone 6 onto my lounge chair. It bounces off and hits the floor. What's one more crack?

Candie's. I need Candie's Fried Chicken.

After calling and ordering chicken for delivery, I slouch into my La-Z-Boy chair and turn on the news. Watching the nightly news has become a tradition of mine, though I don't care much for politics. It's the petite brunette with piercing steel-gray eyes that used to melt me like butter on a biscuit when they looked at me. She appears now and then, giving updates about her candidate's campaign happening. She's who I care about. Well, it's not so much as care *for* her as it's keeping *tabs* on her so no one in town surprises me with information on her. Small-town people—their meddling, gossiping, and all that.

The chicken arrives, and then I dig in. I crave a cold beer, but I promised Pops I'd never drink alcohol in a bad mood. He and Mom would be proud of the decision to refrain if they were still here.

The news has been covering Darcy Marshall, and by default my ex-fiancée, all evening, flashing pictures of her in all different sorts of professional, appealing outfits. A picture of her smiling, standing next to Darcy Marshall covers the screen, and then a younger picture of her looking like the woman I once knew appears. The woman I got down on one knee for. And those little glimpses of my ex-fiancée send me reaching for more of Candie's Fried Chicken. Muttering a string of grumblings, I turn off the television wondering why I even submit myself to this torture. I dig around for my phone, find it under my butt, and search for my best friend

Jared's name. It's easy because I keep all my contacts listed by first initial and last name. But when I go to start texting, a message pops up in his thread.

J. Helms: Don't watch the news tonight.

Me: Too late.

J. Helms: On my way. Bringing the gloves.

I walk out to the garage, which I turned into a shabby makeshift boxing ring—a pad of black mats on the floor—a couple of years ago. I turn on my boxing playlist, which is filled with 70s-80s classic rock, and cringe when "Crying" by Aerosmith blares over the speakers. It's the soundtrack of the last ten years of my life. I'm wrapping my wrists in athletic tape when Jared walks in. He looks me over, debating whether to address the elephant in the room, I presume. Jared is the scariest of men—big, brawny, and looks as if he could murder you when he isn't smiling. But I know him. He is a big softy under all the layers of muscle and murderous stares.

"So, you saw her tonight," Jared prods, stripping his shirt away and beginning to wrap his wrists. I make a sound somewhere between a grunt and growl, completely ignoring the question. My animal instincts have taken over. Fight first. Talk later.

"I'll take that as a yes," Jared mumbles. Slapping his mouthguard in and slipping on his gloves, he meets me in the ring.

We circle each other a few times before a small smile tugs at the corner of Jared's lips. This is Jared's tell for throwing the first punch, so I slip out of the way and follow with my own front punch to the left shoulder. *Niiiice,* I think to myself, letting my guard down a bit. He recovers quickly from the punch, landing his own on my chest. We go back and forth with a few more punches, each one releasing pent-up frustration. I land another punch to his jaw to pay him back for the one he delivered to me. The punch throws him off balance. I use the advantage and take out his wobbling legs, nailing him to the ground. I am on top of Jared instantly. *Holy heck! I may win tonight.* I feel my chest swell because I have never won a match against the boxing champ himself. Jared looks like he is getting ready to tap out. I let my grip ease a little, preparing to gloat. I think I just beat Jared for the—*agh!* I'm suddenly underneath Jared, and his arm has found its rightful place at my throat. There is no getting out of this without dying of suffocation. *Curse our made-up rules.* I slap my hand against the matted floor three violent times and feel a rush of air fill my lungs.

"You couldn't let me win...just tonight?" I choke out, still catching my breath.

"Nope. Never." Jared smirks as he offers his hand to help me up. I wipe a sheen of sweat from my face.

"You don't get to gloat when you win against me," I manage to say, still letting air fill and circulate within my lungs.

"I get to gloat every time I win," he retorts. "Even if it's against a baby cub like you." He is the one who boxes for money. I do it to release my frustration. You know, as an alternative to sitting in front of my TV stuffing my face with greasy food, which was threatening to make a reappearance after that round.

He asks if I want to go another round, which I vehemently decline, and we head back into the living room. One round is enough with a professional.

"Okay, bud. It's time to spill," Jared states as he plops down on the reclining chair. For a man who is like a butterfly in the ring, slipping, dodging, and striking, he moves about in everyday life like a sluggish ogre.

"I just saw Stella on the news, no big deal," I reply casually, occupying myself with wiping down the kitchen countertops.

"Dude. You're cleaning. You don't clean unless you're trying to take your mind off something. What's going on?" Jared asks with a knowing smirk.

I place both hands flat against the kitchen counter. "She's coming back for a few weeks, and Stone asked me to be the one to pick her up," I spill. "In Jackson." Jared's cringe echoes my thoughts.

"Ouch man, that's rough. When?"

"Tomorrow evening. I'm leaving right after school dismisses."

"I'd volunteer for you, but I have a big match."

"It's the thought," I say, knowing good and well he would have. Time to change the subject. "So, are you still down for helping with the boys' and girls' soccer booth at the (Not So) Winter Wonderland on the 21st?"

I dread this stupid booth every year, but as head coach of the boys' soccer team, I'm roped in. Dasher Valley puts on a large Christmas festival every year right before Christmas Eve. The name stemmed from the idea that it never snows in Mississippi, but we still create an atmosphere of Christmas spirit that leaves many in wonder of the season. Dasher Valley High School "strongly suggests" that all sports teams and clubs run a booth to help fundraise for their activities. At least we do the same theme every year: *Frozen's* Winter Extravaganza, complete with reindeer games and all.

Except this year is different. The position of Athletic Director at Dasher Valley High is opening, and my eyes are tracking it closer than the kids track Santa on the television. To prove my management skills (and not just as a kick-butt coach) to the Board and Principal Mitchell, I volunteered to coordinate the entire Athletic Department's booths and still run our soccer booth. Well, with the help of Saint Jared, of course.

"Wouldn't miss it!" I don't miss the blush creeping up his neck.

"Ask the woman out already, Jared." Every year, for the past five years that I've done the festival, he has "helped" me. By help I mean he stood behind my booth and ogled Gracie Jameson working Honey's Bakery and Café diagonal to us. "Five years is a long time of pining," I state, moving to sit on the couch next to the recliner with the TV remote in hand.

"Shut up, dude." Jared swipes the remote from me. "You've been sulking and pining for ten."

To which I have no verbal comeback because it's true.

THREE

STELLA

"Safe travels! Don't forget about me back in Hick Town." Hayden squeezes me tight. I should be upset at her use of language toward my home state, but she's not wrong. Part of me wonders if that accent I've worked so hard to rid myself of will reappear like it never left the moment I fly across the state line.

Though I didn't tell Hayden much about why I've been obsessively cleaning, throwing myself deeper into work than usual, and biting my fingernails to the nubs, she saw it all and wouldn't let me leave without telling her the basics: I have an old fling (though he was totally more than that) back home that I'm not looking forward to seeing. She did offer to come with me, but I told her she needed to stay close to Darcy and this was something I had to do alone. I haven't been home in ten years, and there are things I need to atone for. I've left it up to God. If *he* is in town and I bump into *him*, I'll take that as my sign to offer myself up as a sacrificial animal ready for atonement like in the Old Testament days. If not, then I'm in the clear for another however many years until I am summoned back to my hometown. Though, if I am successful on this trip, I will never have to return except to slip in and out to visit Mama in assisted living care. My heart leaps at the thought of leaving my past behind me for good.

God obviously knows which option I want. I'm sure He will oblige. He's held me through my plans so far.

"I love you. Thank you for being you." I wrap Hayden in a bear hug as we sway back and forth.

"I love you too. Don't go falling in love with any old flings." She laughs against my ear, and my stomach quivers. "Actually, you could use some love. Go ahead." I shift away, looking anywhere but at Hayden. I never told her specifically about *him*... The one my heart was intended for. She doesn't know the depths to which that *fling* lasted.

After collecting myself, I give her one last hug and we part ways.

I make my way to the front counter to check in. Once I make it through the TSA, I grab a Snickers candy bar and water for the flight. I take a bite and realize I haven't treated myself to snacks often enough. Being a woman in the political world is tough. My southern roots involved carb-loaded home-cooked meals, but to compete in New York, I had to drop a few pounds. A man didn't tend to jump at the thought of a woman managing his campaign, but if the woman looked good and had wits to her... Game over. So I made myself look good so that the men would see my brains. It is what it is.

My phone buzzes, pulling me out of my thoughts. I see a Snapchat from Gracie Jameson, my best friend back in Mississippi. I open it, and it's a message with a plane emoji and a question mark. I snap a picture of me with the gate in the background. Immediately, she sends back a picture of her busy café, saying she is sorry she can't pick me up. Licking my lips, I remember the gingerbread cookies she sent me a few weeks ago. I am *so* ready for more of those. With a Cheshire Cat smile, I take another picture and tell her how it's fine, that I'll get a rental, and how excited I am to finally see her business—Honey's Bakery and Café—in person.

They announce my flight is boarding, and my stomach churns again. I shove the feelings down, tuck my phone away, and clutch my ticket in my hand. Taking one last breath, I square my shoulders as if preparing for battle. Here goes nothing.

Making my way up the onboarding ramp and into the plane, I find my seat. *Hooray for window seats!* I won't feel claustrophobic or trapped. I throw my carry-on bag into the compartment above me and settle into my seat. After popping in my Air Pods, I send out a few emails before switching my phone to Airplane mode. The recording plays, letting us know we are preparing for takeoff. My thoughts flick back to Mama as I lean back in my window seat listening to Loretta Lynn's "Country Christmas." When I hear that country twang come through my headphones, I am back in Mama's arms as she rocks me to sleep. The plane takes off, and the Dramamine I took earlier is kicking in right on time.

I let thoughts of her, Dasher Valley at Christmas, and haunting memories from the Ghost of Christmas Past wisp me off to sleep.

I gather my carry-on items from beneath my feet, shaking the sleep away, as the plane prepares for landing. New York to Mississippi isn't a long flight, but it was just long enough for a power nap. I'm juiced up and ready to help Mama out with whatever she needs. And by that, I mean I am ready to convince the stubborn woman to get the help she needs by moving into Heritage Assisted Living Care. I am laser-focused. This year's Christmas agenda: persuade Mama and promote Darcy Marshall.

The plane lands, and we're dismissed. The door opens, and I immediately regret wearing my cream chunky sweater and leggings. It may as well be May and not December. Mississippi is warm and humid for Christmas. It's rare that there's a cold blast, and you could probably spot Bigfoot before you see snow. I suck it up and make my way to baggage claim, the humidity already claiming my straightened hair for its own.

I grab my luggage and make my way toward the rental cars where I called in advance to book one. There is no way Mama could pick me up in her condition, so I get to have the two-and-a-half-hour drive alone to myself. I'm looking forward to blasting Taylor Swift and singing at the top of my lungs while dancing behind the wheel. Just kidding. I don't dance while driving (I totally do). That's not safe.

"A-hem," a man clears his throat behind me. Why so loud? Gross.

My phone vibrates in my leggings (yay for leggings with pockets), so I click my earpiece on and answer. "This is Harper, go ahead," I say, strictly business. When I don't look at the caller first, I always answer professionally. That lesson was learned the hard way when I thought my brother was calling but it was the state senator I was trying to get elected at the time.

"Hey, seester." It's safely my brother this time.

"'Sup, bro? I just landed in Jackson."

"Great! Hey, I sent someone to pick you up so that you didn't have to—"

"A-HEM," the man clears his throat again, louder this time. I take a couple of steps forward, but the man says my name, stopping me in my tracks.

How in the world did I bump into someone I know so fast? *Why, God?* I whip around with a fake smile, prepared for a brief, pleasant greeting. But one look at the man and I drop every single one of my bags.

Lucas Grady is standing right in front of me with a look that could (and might) kill me. I don't know why his angry look is my favorite (was my favorite, I can't lay claims to him now), but under that gaze, my body lights up like fireworks at the town's annual Fourth of July display, while a wave of nausea rolls over me. I wasn't supposed to see him—if at all—until I had my apology ready. But how do you apologize for abandoning an engagement without so much as a note saying goodbye? *Oh hey. Sorry about that. I was foolish and only eighteen. We all good?*

The man before me has changed since I left the diamond ring he slid onto my finger sitting on his nightstand the night I left Mississippi for Boston and Harvard. Though Lucas is still wearing faded jeans and a flannel, he fills them out more. A lot more. His brown hair still has a slight curl, the color of the freshly watered, tilled soil on his family's farm, which frames his face at all the right angles. A trimmed beard matching his hair color lines his cheeks and chin, connecting above his full lips... *Oh heavens,* I'm in trouble.

"Stone, I have to..." I hang up the phone by clicking my earpiece. *Lucas is standing in front of me. The man I left.* The thought sets in, and my chest constricts. *No, not here.* Though my breath becomes jagged, I close my eyes and inhale. Exhale. A few more rounds of breathing and I'm okay.

I think. I open my eyes again.

I try to swallow the rock in my throat as topaz-colored eyes bore into mine with an intensity that has me taking a few steps back, stepping on the edge of one of my bags.

Gravity does the rest.

My ankle gives way with a nauseating POP, and I find myself lying on the cold, hard ground.

Thank you, Taylor Swift. Lucas Grady is going be T-R-O-U-B-L-E indeed.

FOUR

LUCAS

When Stella Harper whipped around to face me—glacier eyes bugged out of her head—I thought she was going to pass out. Or have an anxiety attack. The way her breaths grew ragged had me thinking the latter. Old feelings of holding her tight while she calmed down, rubbing circles on her back, and whispering into her ear came flooding back for a moment. But then, she took a couple of steps back, tripping over her many bags, and fell flat on her back. No matter how much I disliked the woman, I couldn't leave her looking unconscious on the airport floor. I *definitely* couldn't leave her on the airport floor while I busted at the seams laughing at the oh-so-sweet moment of God-given revenge.

I walk to her side, bending down to...well, I don't know what I'm planning to do. Her chest is rising and falling, so she's breathing. Several people have wandered over to us—some recording, others seeming like they want to help but don't know what to do. Her eyes flutter open, and she lets out a massive groan.

"She's fine. Just a little clumsy. I've got her." I dismiss the on-lookers. Not that they all magically disappear. I guess we're reuniting after ten grueling years with an audience.

Stella groans again as she begins to sit up, but then she sways a little before collapsing back to the ground. In closer proximity and prepared this time, I catch her, hands cradling the back of her head. My fingers instinctively weave into her wavy, chestnut brown hair. And it's there on that airport floor, holding Stella Harper in my arms after an eternity, though it feels like not a moment removed, that I remember every aching, heart-wrenching moment of the day I woke up, rolled over on my side, and saw the diamond ring I gave her sitting on my nightstand. No explanation. No note. No phone call. Memories I've worked day in and day out to suppress overload my system, confusing my brain. I'm ticked at her; that emotion is strong. But a few tiny cells in my body are reveling in the feel of her hair between my fingers.

I gently lower her head back to the ground before stripping off my flannel and folding it into a pillow. Tucking a hand under her head and lifting, I slip the homemade pillow beneath her head and run my fingers through her frizzy hair.

Apparently, the few tiny cells are winning out.

"Lucas." She says my name in a dazed, breathy tone. My knees feel a little weak at my name on her lips. A sound that's only haunted my dreams. I'm glad I'm already on my knees beside her or else I'd be falling over, too.

"What's with all the bags?" I ask, finally finding the will to speak up. She brings her hands over her eyes. Mascara smears under her eyes and across her cheeks as she fervently rubs her eyes. They grow wide as her face turns tomato red.

"I'm a woman," she snaps. Yep, she's coming back around. "I need things." Her attitude slaps me out of my doting, and I'm back to being fully ticked.

"I just want to thank your..." I take a moment to count the bags. "Five bags." I act like I'm on an award show accepting a grand trophy. "They made my day. Payback's a...well, you know." I shrug with a satisfied smile at the scowl contorting her face.

She mumbles words I'm positive are curses, her face somehow growing redder. Probably with anger over embarrassment. "What are you doing here?"

"Transporting you to Marian's," I state. "Won the short end of the stick draw." She inches herself up, so I jump back to my feet and then reach down to pick my flannel up off the ground.

"I'm surprised you were even part of the draw," she replies after sitting upright, leaning against a column. Her head rolls back to rest against the structure. The sweater she wears slides down, revealing a bare shoulder. My eyes trace her fawn-colored skin from the roundness of her shoulder, up her tilted, slender neck, until the traitors land on parted pink lips.

Snap out of it, Lucas. You don't particularly like her right now. And she isn't yours to look at like that anymore.

"Stone tricked me," I say. "Your brother asked me with his..."

"Puppy dog eyes," we say in unison. Great. We're already completing each other's sentences again.

I offer a hand to help her off the floor and our eyes lock. The misty gray eyes that have haunted my dreams stare back at me in real life. A montage of moments staring into those eyes assaults me unbidden. I fight the urge to drown in those fathomless grays.

Maybe she wants to drown me? She is snippy. Though I guess I'd be snippy, too, if I'd just fallen flat on my butt in front of my ex-...well, her. If I can't stand her then maybe it's mutual? Whatever the case, I did nothing wrong. She probably concocted something wrong I did to her in her mind for her to just up and leave like that.

Seeing her in person has shown me just how not over her I am. How much anger I still hold toward her for what she did. I shouldn't feel this way. It was ten years ago. I'm a grown man who should have moved on with his life. But I haven't, and that's the problem. She's moved on, and I've been pining my existence away watching cable news, stuffing my face with greasy fried chicken, and getting my butt kicked by an oversized professional boxer.

Stella takes my hand after a moment, but I quickly realize she can't put weight on her left ankle. She looks pitiful, sitting on the dirty airport floor like an injured doe on the side of the road. I can't help but want to walk out, leaving her in a helpless, confused state. Just as she left me.

But I won't.

Because I'm a gentleman.

And because Marian Harper would murder me for leaving her daughter stranded in a crowded airport.

I release her hand and leave her side without a word in search of a medic. I won't get revenge and hurt her the way she hurt me, but who says I can't make her sweat it out a bit?

I find a medic rather quickly because a Good Samaritan who saw the incident had already sought one out. *So much for making her sweat it out,* I huff. I notice two chairs sitting against a wall and head over to snag them while Stella recounts what happened to the medic.

I set the chairs down facing each other before offering a hand down to help Stella up. She eyes me warily like I'll drop her hand and walk off again.

"Take my hand, Stella. You need the help." She shakes her head. "All right," I say, gesturing to the chair. Go ahead, Miss Can-Do-It-Herself.

After several attempts of trying to stand like a newborn calf trying to find its legs, and me not bothering to suppress my laughter, she finally caves.

"I can't get up on my own," Stella admits, irritation lacing her voice. She has always been Miss Independent, and New York City likely reinforced that particular trait ten times over since she's been there.

"Ask me nicely, and I'll see what I can do." I cross my arms, waiting.

"Please," she snaps.

"Mmm, not good enough." My lips twitch in the corners as I try to maintain a blank stare.

"With a cherry on top?" she hisses through clenched teeth.

"Only snakes hiss, Stella. And snakes aren't very nice. Try again."

"I work in the viper pit," she scoffs. "I know how to handle a snake. And I also know how to be one when needed."

Her words take me by surprise. "Yeah, it was a pretty snakish move. What you did ten years ago." The words pass through my own set of clenched teeth before I can stop them. Her eyes grow wide before softening into something that looks a lot like sorrow. She turns her face away from me.

Why is she sad? She's the one who left.

"I guess it was," she whispers. Once again, my brain feels like that one episode of SpongeBob where the little SpongeBobs are running around his mind setting important memos and memories to fire. Chaos and confusion reign as I battle between the sorrow written on her face and the choice she made all those years ago.

Without another word, and an apparent lapse of a sound mind, I bend down and scoop her up into my arms. Another point for my unresolved feelings for my ex-fiancée. Why didn't I offer a hand again? Like a normal guy? A hint of the classic vanilla perfume she wears falls over me. Her lips shine with gloss, and I can't help but wonder if it still tastes like vanilla cake.

It's nice to know she hasn't departed from her signature scent. A scent that has me salivating like a dog at the mere hint of it.

I take that back.

I wish she was wearing a garlic necklace with onion lip gloss.

Because I don't want to want her like I do at this moment—her body nested perfectly against my chest, my heart pounding like a jackhammer, our faces mere inches from each other. Both holding our breaths.

I quickly set her down in the chair, taking a few steps back to free myself of her. *She left you*, I remind myself. *Nothing is like it used to be. It never will be. You can't stand her, and she obviously doesn't want you. She left.*

The medic examines her pupils and then moves to check her ankle. After placing Stella's ankle in the chair, the medic rolls up Stella's leggings and takes off her white slip-on shoe. Something tugs at my heart with each whimper and sharp intake of breath at the medic's touches.

She's suffering, and it causes a phantom ache in my chest.

I take a few steps closer to get a better look, and sweet gravy! Her swollen ankle is turning various shades of blue, purple, and black.

"Definitely sprained, but could be broken," the medic says as she finishes torturing Stella with every slight touch. "I recommend getting an x-ray as soon as possible." Stella groans, bringing her hands to her face to wipe her eyes again.

Except this time, there are actual tears.

"I'll take her tomorrow morning bright and early to get it looked at," I promise the medic. I will have to because Marian can't drive, and Stone isn't home. But I won't make it fun. It'll be cutting into my prep time for the (Not So) Winter Wonderland.

"Her vitals are good, and I do not see any signs of a concussion. Have her take ibuprofen for the headache. Check on her every few hours tonight just to be sure."

"Oh, I don't—" I begin when Stella interrupts.

"We don't live together," Stella says, her eyes flicking between me and the medic.

"Is there anyone to tend to her tonight?" the medic asks. "I highly recommend someone staying with her in case of a concussion." When you put it that way...

"Of course. I'll make sure she is set up with everything she needs." But there is no way Marian can stay up to check on Stella. Looks like I'm having a sleepover at the Harper House tonight with my ex-fiancée.

"Am I good to go now?" Stella asks the medic in a shaky voice.

"Let me wrap your ankle and get a wheelchair."

"No, no. I don't need a wheelchair." She shakes her head several times.

"You do. I cannot carry your five bags and you at the same time." Her eyes grow wide for a moment as she considers. I give my ultimatum. "You can sit here sulking like a sad puppy while I load your bags and pull the truck around, or you can get your butt in a wheelchair, carry a few bags, and escape the phone cameras that have been on you this whole time." She frantically looks around and spots the two lingering people with phones up and trained on us.

"Fine," she surrenders. "I better not be TikTok viral in the morning. Mr. Marshall will kill me."

Without saying another word to each other, I find myself in a position I never imagined I'd be in—wheeling Stella Harper with her laptop bag and purse in her lap out of the airport, while pulling two rolling bags and carrying her duffle bag across my body.

The woman has baggage for sure.

FIVE

STELLA

I envision God, all High and Mighty in the clouds looking down on my life. He saw me in New York living my best life. He saw Lucas in Mississippi doing...well, I don't know what Lucas has been up to other than the occasional Instagram stalk I do like a proper ex-fiancée.

Anyway, God mischievously rubbed His hands together, warming them up for when He plucked me right out of New York with one hand and grabbed Lucas kicking and screaming (how I imagine his phone call with Stone went) with the other.

Setting us down in the middle of the crowded Jackson airport.

"Have a good show, my children," God whispered as He stifled a laugh, prodding us along to play out the situation He just created.

One that involved a blush-inducing, ankle-murdering, pride-stealing, dreadful way to meet-your-ex-fiancé-after-ten-years circumstance.

Thanks, God. I thought we had a deal. I mentally screech, then chuckle under my breath. I know God cares and is full of love. But it's fun to try and figure out His ways and watch as He proves me wrong over and over again.

Now, I'm sitting in Lucas's lily pad green beat-up truck, leaning as far away from him as possible while I gaze out the passenger window. How is this truck still running? Pops, what he called his father, gave it to him as a graduation gift. It retains a musty scent from one too many mud dives. A scent I oddly missed.

There is no room to prop my now-wrapped ankle in this two-door truck, so it's dangling and throbbing. A constant reminder of my humiliating run-in with Lucas freaking Grady.

All the romance novels and movies say moments like that—where you meet your ex-fiancé again after ten years—are supposed to be cute.

That atrocity was nothing but a snippet from a Stephen King novel if you ask me.

We can't hold a conversation, not that either of us is trying much. Lucas has one hand on the wheel, the other sitting in his lap the way a schoolboy hints he wants to hold his girlfriend's hand at the movies. Except I'm positive he wants absolutely nothing to do with my hand. The scowl across his face proves my thought correct. *Quit staring at him like he's an alien, Stella.*

But here I am, memorizing the new lines around his eyes, forehead, and mouth. Lucas has aged like fine wine. His hands look bigger than I remember holding the wheel of this old truck, and the muscles in his arms flex as he tightens and loosens his grip. Gone is the boy who asked to marry me. Beside me is a grown man who slightly resembles the Ole Spice #FlannelFresh lumberjack man.

I want to ask Lucas if he has a girlfriend or a new—gulp—fiancée. I don't know why I stumbled on the word. He's not married because I'd commissioned Gracie to let me know if *that* happened a long time ago. Though, I made her promise not to tell me about new girlfriends he might acquire. I need to know these things, as old friends, you know? I wonder if his favorite color is still the orange color of the sunset or if his favorite food is still Candie's Fried Chicken. What gym is he using now? Because it's paying off. I want to know how he's faring since his parents died in that car crash a few years ago.

I decide to woman-up and ask him one of the many questions occupying my mind.

"Mama told me about what happened with your parents after I...well, you know." Of course, I word-vomit the worst possible question to start with. And it's more of a statement than a question. *Smooth Stella. Way to use your top-notch political speech training.*

I turn my body toward him. I don't just need him to talk about this *with* me. I need it *for* me. His parents were my second set. After my Dad died when I was fifteen, Pops became my only earthly father figure.

Lucas places the other hand on the wheel and his grip clenches tight enough that veins pop up and down his tanned, muscular arms. His dark eyebrows knit together, the typically warm caramel color of his eyes shading over to a burnt sunset.

"It was too hard for me to come. I should have, but I couldn't. I am... I'm sorry." I got the funeral invitation. Mama called. Stone called. Jared Helms, Lucas's best friend, called. Gracie called. I couldn't do it. I couldn't bring myself to face him after the way I left. My reason for leaving was unbelievably silly and immature. But that thought didn't settle in my brain until I finished Harvard. I had cut the ties and there was no use in weaving the frayed edges back together.

His grip loosens as he turns his head to face me, taking in a deep breath. And for a brief second, he lets his guard down, and I get a full view of the grief in his eyes.

"It's okay," he says with a single nod, letting his breath out. He contorts his face back into a scowl that would challenge Scrooge himself. I know I left him, but that was ten years ago. Could he have held anger the same way I've held shame all this time?

We spend the rest of the ride in a settled silence. I mentally kick myself for not holding my tongue and going straight for the eight-ball shot of questions. But that's the thing. It just came out. My usual calm and collected, strategic, poised self slipped. I can't let that happen again.

After a long and quiet two-and-a-half-hour drive, we pull up to the back porch of my childhood home. I worry my frizzy hair between two fingers, static taking hold. The stringed porch lights illuminate the immediate surroundings of the small, cabin-esque house. The grass is mowed and the flower bed in front of the porch is pruned. Stone must have mowed and cleaned up the yard before heading back to college on his last visit.

But where are all the Christmas lights and decorations?

Lucas is opening my door and scooping me out of his truck before I realized he was even out of the truck. My arms instinctively fold around his neck as he holds me like a groom carrying his bride across the threshold. My body is pressed tight against his chest. He still smells like mint and fresh earth and sunshine. I hate that I know this is just how he smells—no cologne or body spray. All Lucas.

I refrain my hands from exploring the new muscles in his chest that were not there the last time he held me this way ten years ago. I mean, Lucas has been spending some serious time in the gym. His chest is hard as a rock beneath my hands. And the flimsy white t-shirt under the open flannel he's wearing stretches tauntingly across his skin, begging me to put my hands flat on his chest like I'm giving him electric cardioversion. The heat from his body is radiating out, warming me from the slight chill in the air. Not New York cold by any means, but Mississippi winter nights still have a certain crisp to them.

The large porch swings are clean, but there is a glass of tea with two lemons sitting on the table between the rocking chairs, drops of water rolling down the sides. Mama must have been out here before it got too cold for her sensitive joints.

Lucas opens the door (while still holding me with one hand!) and gently contorts our bodies to fit through the small door frame. I'm smushed against this man in all the right places. He feels like True North.

Home.

I didn't realize I was missing home.

Lucas sets me down on the old tan couch I spent many nights cuddling him on once upon a time.

"Marian. I got you a surprise," Lucas calls, walking on a mission across the kitchen and toward her room like he's going to pick her up and set her down on the couch next. I look around the living room—it's clean but bare. Where is the Douglas Fir tree? Where is the fireplace mantle nativity scene? Where are the stockings that Mama has used for Stone and me for as long as I can remember?

Mama hobbles into the living room holding on tight to Lucas's arm for support, a cane in the other hand. My breath catches at the sight of her.

Mama's always been a beautiful woman. I've seen pictures of her in her younger years, and she looked like one of those girls who made everyone else's self-esteem take a hit when she walked into a room. She is every bit as beautiful now, but it's a broken beauty. Her eyes are still young and bright, mimicking my own. She's shorter and the wrinkles in her face and hands are deeper than ever. Oh, those hands...

Her fingers are no longer straight and a couple of them seem to cross over one another. No wonder she cannot use them anymore. Her toes reflect her fingers, though thankfully not as extreme. She walks toward me slowly, her knees never fully straightening out. Rheumatoid has laid its claim to her body, taking over every inch.

But not her spirit.

"My baby girl!" she squeals, continuing to make her way to me, breaking free of Lucas's grip. "Oh, you're finally home!" I push myself off the couch to embrace her in my arms. I feel like Olaf from *Frozen*—really loving this warm hug thing. "This is the best Christmas."

"Hey Mama," I whisper against her ear, sinking into her and pulling her tight against me. She feels so fragile, but I know how strong she is.

Lucas clears his throat before stepping around us.

"All right, Harper women. I'm going to haul Stella's apartment in here really quick." He says that last part with a grumble. I ignore his grumblings and continue to cling to Mama like she's a bomb that'll blow if I let go.

"I've missed you," we both say at the same time, laughing through tears. And just like in the truck with Lucas, I have a million and five questions I want to ask her. Gosh, I've missed her physical presence. FaceTime does no justification for being present with Mama, inhaling her sweet scent that smells suspiciously of chocolate chip cookies.

I lean away from the hug but leave my hands resting on her biceps.

"Have you been eating cookies?" I ask, giving her my interrogation eyebrow raise. My good leg is burning with the full weight of my body, but I push through because Mama is standing right in front of me, and I don't want to let her go.

"Yes, I have." She has not an ounce of sorrow or regret. She looks at me now, taking me in. But then she looks down and notices I'm on one leg. "Why are you standing on one leg, why is your foot wrapped, and where is your shoe?"

"Mama! You have to keep your sugar in check!" I spout, ignoring her inquiry about my foot. It sounds ridiculous to question chocolate chip cookies as I look over her frail, thin frame. But Type 1 Diabetes couldn't care less about your weight.

"Hogwash," she spits the words at me. "I am a fifty-two-year-old woman who can eat whatever I want, do whatever I want, and *whom*ever I want."

"MAMA!" I cover my face with my hands. Do you know that line where your mama becomes your best friend as well as your mama? We crossed that line when I was seventeen and she discovered she could embarrass me by making sexualized jokes in the face of my innocence. She's in a fit of giggles at making my face flush when Lucas comes back in like a pack mule with Louis Vuitton suitcases and bags in haul.

"Now what's wrong with you? Besides looking pencil-thin. Do they feed you in that city of yours?"

I motion for Mama to take a seat on the couch before easing down beside her, oh so very careful to not nudge my foot.

"Oh, it's nothing. Just a little sprain. Of course, I eat, just not fried—"

"I'll be taking her to the clinic to get that ankle of hers X-rayed bright and early," Lucas interrupts, throwing my bags down on the floor beside the couch. I shoot a pair of daggers his way. Those travel bags might be the most expensive thing I own since I travel so much for my job. Well, besides my Louboutin heels. Every credible woman in politics owns a pair of the red outsole stilettos.

"X-ray?!" Mama exclaims. "Why do you need an X-ray? Is it that bad? You've had plenty of sprains in the past." Mama is always one to avoid the doctor if she can. Which is probably why the RA went unnoticed for so long.

"Mama's right," I counter. The determination in his eyes says otherwise, but I continue, "No need for a doctor. I'll be fine."

"You're not fine. You can hardly walk. Not a drastic change from *before* the Suitcase Incident." The scowl reaches his eyes. While it's true that I am a well-known klutz, I embrace it. It's part of my charm. But I am stuck on the way he says "suitcase incident" like our reuniting moment has an official title now. Why do I like it?

"The Suitcase Incident?" Mama's accent is thick when she is pushing for information.

Lucas and I look at each other and a smile incrementally pulls across his face, giving him full-on Grinch vibes. What the heck?

"Well, Marian, what happened was..." His wicked smile broadens as he tells his version of the Suitcase Incident. "I saw Miss Harper here, strolling through the airport like she owned the place. I hollered her name and she whipped around, coming face to face with her very own *extremely handsome* Ghost of Christmas Past." He raises one eyebrow and tilts his head in my direction as if to challenge reality. *Challenge accepted.*

"No, Mama. He's got it *all* wrong." I sneer. "I was talking to Stone when some man kept clearing his throat behind me—we all know how gross that is." I glare at him. But what *did* happen next? He said my name, my heart dropped to hell, I dropped my bags and then did what I do best—trip. *Yeah, that's a real winner of an argument on your end.*

"Go on, Stella…" I want to wipe the smirk off his pretty face. But I have no manipulated story that paints me in a flattering light. I sigh, defeated.

Lucas: One.

Stella: Zero.

"And that's why I'm taking Stella bright and early to go to the clinic. I've got to stay here tonight and check in on her every couple of hours for a concussion or something like that," he finally finishes.

"You don't have to do all that, Lucas," Mama pushes back. Points for Marian Harper!

"You can't check on her because of the stairs. I won't take no for an answer because I care about you, Marian."

"I can manage for one night," she says. "I do appreciate the concern over Stella, though."

"I'm concerned about *you,* Marian." His voice is ice. "Not Stella."

"Um, guys." I clear my throat. "I can just sleep on the couch tonight." Lucas looks taken aback for a moment, but then his face contorts into the grimace he has been flaunting all evening.

"I didn't think an uppity political princess like you would be humble enough for the couch." Lucas curls his lips while heat courses through my veins. How dare he treat me this way! Sure, I left. But that was ten years ago. He is the one who said those awful words to me and demeaned my dream—my calling. And I've been feeling guilty for leaving…ha!

"Guess you don't know me at all then." I cross my arms, trying not to let him see how much his opinion of me hurts. I've worked my tail off for the life I live, and he has no right to make such assumptions about me. Here I was ogling him. No more!

"Guess not." He stares back at me. "Either way, I'm staying here tonight because Marian doesn't need to be worrying about you all night."

"Mama, tell him we are fine," I plead. If anyone can get the man out of the house, it's her.

"Sweetie," she begins with a tone that signals my defeat. "I would feel better if he stayed. In case you need something, and I can't get to you in time."

The smirk plastering Lucas's face has my blood boiling. The problem? I can't figure out if it is because I want to punch him or kiss him. He may be getting under my skin, but that doesn't mean his sexy smirk isn't calling my lips to his like a moth to a flame.

"*You* are sleeping on the couch then," I state, crossing my arms.

"He can use Stone's room," Mama nods toward the stairs, a sweet, sly smile decorating her face. "That way he'll be a little closer to you if you need him." I send dagger eyes at her as I finally catch on to her game. Typical Mama. Never on the side of her only daughter.

"Great idea, Marian." Lucas claps his hands together with a tilt of his head. It's the look of a man who intends to wake me up for the sheer pleasure of annoying me every two hours on the dot tonight.

"As much as I want to stay up and talk with you, baby girl," Mama says between a series of yawns, "it's past my bedtime. I'm so happy you're home and spending Christmas with me." She hugs me one last time, and I melt like chocolate into the warmth of her arms. I should have braced myself for the potential of her trying to set Lucas and me back up the moment I realized he was bringing me home. I'll have to throw up several defenses against her strikes. Just call me Donald Trump. I'm building my big, beautiful wall.

Lucas helps Mama up from the couch, and I'm continually surprised that she is letting him help so much. She must truly be struggling. This only heightens my drive to get her real help and out of the hands of Lucas Grady.

"I'll haul your luggage up to your room and will be back down for you," he says, running a hand through his shaggy, still slightly curled, dark roast coffee hair and walking back into the living room. He begins to gather my bags, and I let him because there was no way I could carry myself and my luggage up the stairs. But the moment he rounds the hallway at the top of the stairs, I push myself up onto my good foot and hop to the edge of the stairs, wincing at each slight jerk of my ankle.

With one hand on the railing, I hop onto the first step. *Whew.* I look up the stairs and choke at the idea of doing this all the way up. It's like I'm climbing Mt. Everest suddenly. Who knew stairs could be so daunting?

Instead, I get on my knees and begin to carry myself up the stairs knee by knee. Still painful, but at least I'm doing it myself. That'll show—

"Uh, Stella," Lucas says from the top of the stairs. I glance up at him through the warm brown cascade of hair covering my face, with a smile that says *See? I can do this! I don't need you, Lucas Grady.*

He crosses his arms and leans against the wall, an amused smile playing on his lips.

"You look..." his arms fall at his side as laughter escapes, "like *The Ring* girl." I should be offended, but my heart leaps at the sound of his genuine laugh. I almost join in, but I remember his coldness only moments ago and the words he told me that flipped my switch to Boston and Harvard rush back—*it's just a silly dream, Stella*. Huffing, I continue up the stairs on my knees. The girl from Mississippi *can* and *did* make something of herself. I'm not helpless.

I reach the top, with Lucas still belly-laughing and standing in my way.

I give him a pointed look that screams *move*, but he stands there like a brick wall incapable of moving. Standing up on my knees at the last step near the top, I splay my hands and push against his thighs.

His laughter halts quicker than a troll commenting on one of Mr. Darcy Marshall's campaign videos, but Lucas still doesn't budge.

I stare at my hands, resting on Lucas's thighs right above his knees. I swallow the lump in my throat, fire roasting my skin like a chestnut. I should move my hands, but the brain signal to move isn't reaching them. Those muscles feel carved and crafted. My hands give an involuntary squeeze as a shudder rips through me.

He steps away, and I fall forward. My hands, thankfully deciding to work again, catch my fall on the top stair. Without looking up at him, I crawl on my hands and knees to my bedroom, cursing under my breath. I must be in *The Ring* because I'm horrified.

"Language," he says, and I glance back to see him standing in my doorway. Lucas fills the door frame, one hand clutching the side of the frame. He raises his eyebrows, unsuccessfully trying to suppress a grin.

"Shut up, Luca!" He flinches a little at my use of his nickname, his grin fading away.

Grabbing the closest pillow on my bed, I chuck it at him with years of pent-up anger, hurt, and heartache behind the throw. He holds his hands up as if surrendering and backs away. I walk on my knees to the door to shut it, and then wobble back to my bed. My ankle is throbbing. I could use a bag of ice and some more ibuprofen right about now.

But since I refuse to call on Lucas, I use all the strength in my arms to hoist myself onto my bed. *Thank you, God, that the bed sits low.*

Tossing my chunky sweater off, I search for relief from the fire burning in my veins—from Lucas and my impromptu workout. Though nothing can help the throbbing pain in my ankle. It's like I feel my heartbeat pounding over the injury. To distract myself, I scroll through TikTok and other social media platforms to see if a video of me falling on the airport floor has become a meme or gif or something. So far, so good.

I try to fall asleep in my sports bra and leggings. Just in case the blankets fall off me in the middle of the night and Lucas comes in. But I'm too uncomfortable—physically and emotionally—to drift off to sleep. Though, I pretend to be when Lucas opens the door to my room to make sure I'm okay. I hear soft footsteps approaching my bed, then they leave after a moment.

When I hear the door click shut, I roll around to find ibuprofen and a glass of water on my nightstand.

SIX

LUCAS

I've spent the past two hours after checking on Stella tossing and turning. I can't seem to find sleep. My phone buzzes, and I wonder who is contacting me at one o'clock in the morning. Through the cracked screen, I see Jared's name pop up.

J. Helms: You up?

Me: Against my will.

J. Helms: How'd it go picking up Stella?

Me: There was a suitcase incident...

Three dots appear, then disappear.

Then he calls me.

"Figured I better call to hear about this so-called suitcase incident," he says as I pick up the phone, his voice strained. "Did the airline lose one and she had a diva fit over it?"

I chuckle, remembering Stella's face as she whipped her head around and caught sight of me. Her expression changed from an irritated scowl to sheer shock quicker than the weather in Mississippi, and then she stumbled backward as if standing three feet from me would cause her to catch the rhinovirus my microbiology students were studying the other day. *As if she'd never been closer than that to me before...*

The thought stirs anger inside me and thrusts me back to reality. I proceed to fill Jared in on the Suitcase Incident.

To my surprise, he laughs a little at the mention of Stella's ankle.

"That's the main reason I wanted to talk to you." He breathes heavily.

"You knew about Stella?" News sure travels fast in a small town like this.

"No, but it's ironic that happened to her because I broke my leg in three places at the match tonight."

"Dude. What happened?" I listen as he tells me about a hulk of a man falling on top of his leg at a weird angle. "Jeez. I'm sorry, bro. Can I do anything to help?"

"Nah, I'm good right now. Gracie was there, you know?" Even through the massive amount of pain I know he must be in, I can hear the smile in his voice.

"Is she playing nurse?" The same way I am with Stella tonight? Except, no suggestions to the statement whatsoever.

"She was. Took me to the hospital, back home, and got the pain meds. Though I'm trying not to use those. I sent her home and told her to stop worrying about me about five minutes ago." He pauses, "And I regret it."

I can't help but laugh.

"When are you going to snag her up?" The man is a goner.

"She saw my eyes produce tears tonight, bro. And she stuck around. I think I'll have to make my move soon,"

"My man." I nod my head in approval though he can't see me.

"As soon as I learn to move on these crutches," he finishes. And just like that, I realize I have lost my main helper for the (Not So) Winter Wonderland festival.

"You focus on getting better," I say, already thinking through a list of people to ask for assistance. "And don't worry about the festival."

"Yeah, no way that's happening."

"It's cool." The coolest. All that work to be done and only me to do it.

"So, how did you feel seeing Stella again?" he asks.

"Dude. Really? You want me to talk about my feelings?"

He ignores my comment. "Does she look different than on the television?"

With a sigh, I oblige the teen girl living within his brute body.

"No. So much better." I hear him "whooping" on the other end of the line. "But just because her looks have changed for the better doesn't mean she has. She's still the person who left me without a word."

"You never know. Why don't you get to know this version of Stella?" Because I'm not suicidal. The way she wrecked me ten years ago is still fresh. I won't let it happen again. I can't.

He must take my lingering silence as an answer because he yawns and murmurs something about needing a pain pill after all. I say a prayer of healing with him over the phone and click off, anxious to get my mind off his comment.

But I kind of find the idea intriguing, not going to lie. However, the monster that flairs up inside of me every time I think of her ring sitting on my nightstand shoves any notion of intrigue rising within me right back down to the bottom of my soul. No, I can't just get to know *this* Stella. I haven't quite let go of the old one yet. I definitely cannot forgive Stella for what she did. I mean, who could? She took my heart and pride, shredding them like cheese on a grater.

I could and I have, a voice echoes in my head. I know it's the Lord speaking to me, urging me to forgive, but I can't hear it right now. It hurt too much. I was doing fine, and then Stone had to call with his dang request to pick her up. He knew I couldn't refuse, not when I knew the joy it would bring Marian to have her daughter home for Christmas. The memories and pain stirred when I saw her standing in the airport. The nauseous churning of my stomach when she whipped her head around and those piercing gray eyes met mine will not be easily forgotten. How could I forgive her for breaking not only our engagement but years' worth of trust and friendship? Sure, we had a fight over her going to school at Harvard. I mean, she had just said yes to marrying me for crying out loud! We needed to sleep on it. But instead of waking up to have a rational discussion about our future, I woke up to never hearing from her again. Even as I sent text after text and rang her phone until her number was changed.

How can I forgive that?

I forgave you, He reminds me.

Not tonight. *I'm sorry, Jesus.*

I reach for the remote and turn on Netflix in an attempt to drown out the thoughts of forgiveness. Because if I'm being honest, I'm still angry with her. No matter how many times I forget that I'm supposed to be mad and lose myself in her eyes and smile instead.

What an eventful Friday the 13th.

Sleep-deprived, grumpy, and dreading having to drive Stella around today, I knock a few times on Marian's front door. I woke up early to go home and change, freshen up, and grab a pair of crutches I had stashed away in the house. If I have to haul Stella around today, might as well make sure she can get around on her own. I have a lot more to do for the festival now that Jared is out of commission, and I can't let her distract me from the opportunity to become Athletic Director.

Marian answers the door with my favorite words. "I have hot biscuits and gravy." Maybe today will go better than expected.

"Smells delicious, Marian." I'm inhaling the heavenly scent.

"Well, get on inside. It's too cold to be standing here with the door open." Marian scoots out of the doorway, and I squeeze myself through the narrow frame. "Thanks for the crutches," she adds. I nod in response. The smell of sausage gravy instantly brightens my mood, and I help myself to three butter biscuits and many scoops of gravy.

"Marian, you've outdone yourself with this breakfast," I manage to say between bites. "Seriously, for a woman with only a handful of functioning fingers, you can cook." She shakes her head, smiling at my comment. Dark humor for the win with Marian Harper.

"My hands are good for many things, thank you very much," she retorts, and a blush creeps up my face. The woman never quits. "Coffee?"

"No ma'am. I'll swing by Honey's for a cup before going up to the school to plan for the festival."

"I'll get you a glass of sweet tea." She's already pulling a pitcher out of the fridge. She pours me a glass and sets it on the table.

"Thank you." I take a sip, enjoying the tea crafted from my little farm. I only have a few plots I take care of on the land remaining, but I keep them up for the memory of my parents. It's enough to supply my favorite people and Honey's with the specialty Grady Family sweet tea.

"Take Stella to Honey's, will you?" Marian's eyes grow wide and round. "I just know she'd love to see Gracie. And the girl can hold her own with coffee."

I remember the days of high school finals. Stella would drink a minimum of five cups of coffee per day. This went on for an entire week, ending with an epic crash where she would sleep for an entire day. The woman was obsessed with her grades and coffee.

"You're not wrong," I comment. "But Jared broke his leg last night and now I have to manage my team's booth at the festival while trying to run the administration side of things for the other sports teams."

"Well, let Stella help you!" She pitches the idea as if it's the most obvious solution in the world.

"No way. She'll just mess everything up."

"Stella plans campaigns. She has gotten powerful men and women elected to public office. She is a well-oiled machine when it comes to planning." I don't have any facts to counter her statement with because she is right. But the last person I want to work with is Stella Harper.

"Marian..." I begin to object, but she cuts me off.

"You'd be stupid not to use her talents, Lucas." I hate to admit she's right.

But she's right. "Fine."

"So, you'll take her to Honey's? I'm sure she's dying to see Gracie. Plus, y'all can do some planning there." Marian uses those familiar puppy dog eyes that are similar to Stone's. With a shrug, I carry on stuffing my face and swigging my tea. I set the glass down a little too hard on the wooden table.

"She hasn't said yes to this," I remind her. Marian flashes me a pleased and satisfied smile as if she's already won.

"Oh, that won't be a problem, son."

With Marian Harper on the case, I'm sure it won't. I'm counting down the days until Stella will go back to New York and let me move on with my life.

"Go wake Stella up, would you? I can't climb those stairs." Again with the puppy dog eyes.

I pinch the bridge of my nose and release a breath.

"Aw heck, Marian. You know I'll do anything for you. But this..." I send daggers her way, "won't end well." I pick up the crutches I'd set beside the table and send a prayer to God as I walk upstairs.

I stand in Stella's doorway, contemplating the best—and safest—way to wake a morning beast. I have to be strategic and plan carefully. I am Steve Irwin stalking the crocodile. This task must be done with a soft, gentle spirit. Or...

I spot a throw pillow on the floor beside her bed. In my defense, she was supposed to be up and ready by now, so don't blame me for what I do next.

After setting the crutches down beside her bed, I pick up the pillow and walk back toward the doorframe prepared to make a quick exit. I chuck the pillow at her serenely sleeping frame and watch her stir for a moment before she brings the blankets over her head like she is a turtle going back into its shell.

Huh. At least one thing hasn't changed—the woman could sleep through a bombing.

And then it hits me. The one way her brother used to wake her up to annoy her. I walk over to his room and find the bell. It's from Japan and is about the length of my forearm. The bell hangs from a stand with a chained hammer attached to it. Stella loves bells.

Adores them. But this one? She would burn it to ash and then bury the ashes to get rid of it...if it wasn't her dad's.

I bring the bell to her room and stand right beside her bed. Pulling the chained hammer to the bell back as far as it will go, I let it fly.

"Diiiinnngggggg," the bell echoes, sending sound vibrations through my ears and to my brain. But that's okay because I get the satisfaction of watching Stella bolt upright in full-on panic with her hair tangled on top of her head. Her hands grope around the bed frantically until she finally pulls out a pair of glasses tucked into the sheets. She needs glasses now? That's new.

She pulls the glasses on and glares fire flames straight from hell at me.

"What the—"

"Tsk tsk, watch your language, Stell Bells." I cut her off, looking her over. "You look nice this morning. Are you planning to go to the clinic like that?" What I don't say is that she does look nice because those black glasses give her a carefree, yet sophisticated, appearance. I like them more than I should, but not enough to give the thought any more credit.

"Ugh, Lucas!" She groans, worry lines creeping over her forehead again. She flings herself back down onto the bed and pulls the blankets up to her chin. I try hard to not like that I am the one bringing flustered heat to her cheeks. But I do.

"Get out of here!"

"What? You don't need help getting ready to go to the clinic?" I want to see just how deep I can make that red blossom. "Because I can be of service." I swoop my hands down my body. I shouldn't be flirting with her. I'm still ticked at her for leaving and for barreling back into my life. But it's like the little boy on the playground who would poke and make fun of her can't resist seizing this moment.

"Oh my gosh, no!" Stella is Christmas-bow red now. "I'll be out in 30 minutes. Just go!" She arms herself with a pillow—locked and loaded.

"Crutches are beside your bed." I nod my head toward the floor where they lie. "That way you don't have to crawl down the stairs like Samara from *The Ring*." She grunts, letting the pillow fly. I duck and shut the door, satisfied that the big city hasn't changed the fact that Stella is a savage in the mornings.

"Thanks for throwing me into the lion's den," I holler from the stairs to Marian who is making a plate of food. She meets my eyes with a wolfish grin.

"Go home, Luca!" I hear Stella yell in response. I smile from the satisfaction of getting under her skin this early in the morning, but her use of the nickname she gave me a long time ago does something weird to my insides. I don't like that I like it.

"Anytime, son."

I take the plate from Marian and place it on the round table for five right where Stella used to always sit.

"Have you eaten, Marian?" I ask, knowing she has.

"Of course, my boy. Not all of us like to sleep until noon like Stella," she retorts. Marian and I spent countless Sundays together eating breakfast and drinking coffee while the rest of her family slumbered away. I always enjoyed Sundays at the Harper house.

A clicking noise coming from the stairs catches my attention, and I watch Stella descending the stairs like a baby giraffe learning how to walk. I stifle a laugh as she takes each stair carefully, placing her crutches down then her good foot as if the slightest wrong move would send her tumbling down.

In her experience, however, it most definitely would.

She finally makes it into the kitchen, and her look of pure concentration on each movement of the crutches throws me over the edge. A sweet pleasure arises in me from the fact that after everything we've been through, she's the one on crutches, face reddened with embarrassment. Serves her right.

"Do you still take breakfast with your coffee? Or did New York rid you of your appetite?" I question Stella, still on a high from irking her.

"Is my name still Stella Harper?" she fires back, and then she shoves a biscuit from the stove into her mouth, crumbs flying everywhere. *Unfortunately,* I think to myself. It should be Stella Grady right now. A fresh wave of gritty anger washes over me, sending my light mood flying right out of the open kitchen window.

"Better eat quick," I say, pointing toward her food on the table. "I've got things to do."

She makes her way to the table slower than the way she came down the stairs. Looking me square in the eyes and sporting a smirk, she sits as if someone hit the slow-motion button, leaning onto her crutches to support her weight. She picks up her fork like she is finally going to start eating, and then she sets it back down. Her eyes never leave mine except to find the fork.

"Forgot to pray." She smiles and bows her head innocently. She spends a minute in prayer over her food with a tiny smirk painted on her lips. I try to interrupt, but she holds up a finger. This goes on for two more minutes as she talks to the Lord with a sweet southern drawl that flows as slowly as molasses.

"The Lord is going to get you for that one, Stella," I mumble through gritted teeth as she finally says amen.

"Stella, would you be a doll and help Lucas plan for the (Not So) Winter Wonderland festival this coming Saturday?" At Marian's question, Stella chokes on the piece of biscuit she'd just bitten off. Then she meets my eyes.

"Did you put her up to this?" Stella snaps at me, waving a half-eaten biscuit in the air.

"Now why in the world would I ask your mother to ask you to help me plan for a festival when the last person I want to spend my time with is you?"

"Because it's your personal flavor of fun to torment me."

"Well, sweetie, if I wanted to have fun with you, I'd just have to pick you up and throw you onto the—" I stop, catching myself before the next word slips through. *Couch.* Blurry is the line between love and loathing. My face grows hot.

I breathe in and out. Once. Twice.

"Jared broke his leg and can't help out anymore. I need this festival to go well," I finally say. I don't tell her what's at stake. She isn't privy to that information in my life anymore.

"You'd be doing the town a big help." Marian pops in, eyeing me. I pull my gaze away from her and focus on Stella. She's deep in thought.

"Fine," she huffs. A laugh escapes my lips at her reaction. The same one I had. "Only for the town."

SEVEN

STELLA

I should take a crutch to his backside. In fact, I think I'll plan on doing that soon. Lucas wakes me up with that obnoxious Japanese bell (I only kept it because it belonged to my dad) and then has the nerve to rush my breakfast? And say stuff he has no business thinking about anymore? I scoff at myself. I know good and well how he was going to finish that sentence. I've had one too many tickle fights that magically transformed into make-out sessions on that couch.

Someone come and get me because I'm going to go bat crazy on this man with my crutches. Lucas Grady is hot—smoldering. But then he is polar ice cold. He's obviously still upset with me for leaving. But there is something lying underneath his angry exterior. And maybe that something will break through before this trip is over. I would love to leave on good terms this go-round.

But I guess I'll have plenty of time to dig underneath his exterior now that I have to help him with the town's Christmas festival.

Why God, why? Though I'm sure His answer is so that I can make amends.

The road rumbles underneath us as he drives me to the clinic. I fought Mama hard about just popping ibuprofen and icing my ankle, but she wouldn't have it. It's impossible to win a battle with Marian Harper. I'll have to be strategic when approaching her about moving into an assisted living home. It will involve a more detailed plan than the campaigns I manage.

Getting tired of the menacing silence, I decide to turn on the radio.

"Santa Baby" by Ariana Grande floats through the truck, and I sing along to myself.

That is until Lucas shuts the radio off.

I reach over and turn it back on, and he shuts it off again. I throw my hands up to say "what in the mess?"

"My truck. My rules. I like the quiet." He stares at me as if I am the bane of his existence. I wonder if he is aware that was a slogan of Robert Foster when he ran for governor of Mississippi? It was a slogan that had women all over the world mocking him, but I secretly liked it. I mean, what woman wouldn't want her man to refuse a woman a ride alone with him in his truck because he was married?

I give up and sit in silence as we stop at the only red light in the town. Staring out of the window, I look around Main Street. It's quiet, but it's only a little after eight in the morning on a Saturday. Tranquil. New York City never sleeps, and I didn't realize how much I'd missed the quiet until this moment.

Who knew Lucas turning off my Christmas music would be so profound?

As he continues to drive, I think back to the night I left. I don't remember much, just the overwhelming feeling of "I've got to get out of here" that settled into my soul a few hours after our engagement. Family and friends started asking us questions such as "Where will you live?" and "How many babies are you going to have?" and "What career field are you looking to enter?"

I panicked. I didn't know the answer to those questions. All I knew was that I loved Lucas with everything inside of me. But I also knew I wanted more. I needed more. A one-red-light town in Mississippi couldn't fulfill my need to change the world. And I was only eighteen.

When I found out I'd gotten into Harvard University the night of our engagement, I felt it was God validating my fears. I didn't want to give up Lucas, though. I thought we could talk it out and make a plan. But his comment that still rings as clear as the day he said it was enough to send me packing that night... *"It's just a silly dream, Stella."* Eighteen-year-old Stella wasn't ready to commit to someone who could say such cruel words to her. At least, they felt that way at the time.

I left without saying goodbye to him. To anyone really, except for Mama, my brother Stone, and my best friend Gracie. I left Mississippi. I left the love of my life. I left my family. I left my best friend. I left the old Stella Harper.

"Dr. Gaines?" I ask Lucas, observing the plaque on the outside of the clinic peeking out from behind four Christmas trees. Dasher Valley does Christmas right. "As in Joseph Gaines from high school?"

"His wife," he corrects, opening the door to the clinic. "Marlee Fletcher married Joseph about a year ago." *Marlee Fletcher...* The name takes me back to food "accidentally" dumped on me in the cafeteria and backhanded compliments about my curvier body shape in skinny jeans.

I become a crutch-running Olympian away from that clinic.

"Stella!" Lucas barks, walking up behind me. He wraps his arms around my waist, picking my feet up and bringing me to a halt. He spins me around so that I'm facing him. My breath hitches. We are chest to chest, and I smell the faint trace of sunshine on his skin. His head is bent and his lips are at my ear. His breath sends tingles through my skin like an electrical current. "We're lucky they're open on Saturdays. Now. Are you going to walk into that clinic by yourself?" His voice is low and gravelly, his drawl like honey. "Or am I carrying you in there tossed over my back like a misbehaving child?"

I could be stubborn so that he will throw me on his back, the thought pops into my head. Where in the Mississippi River did that thought come from?!

With the little dignity I have left, I nod my head and he releases me from his southern spell. The men just don't talk like that up north. The tingles fade slowly, and I face the fact that I have to see my high school nemesis.

Time to refocus. I am the new and improved, successful Stella Harper—I concede and hobble my way into Hell's Hospital.

I'm tapping my good foot a mile a minute while my other remains limp, propped in the cushioned chair Lucas fetched for me. He's been eyeing the thick, fuzzy sock covering my left foot. It was too swollen to stuff into my sneakers today, so I opted for a leopard print number with two fuzzy balls hanging from the side, complete with candy canes in a heart shape on the front. I thought it was cute, even though it severely clashed with my oversized plaid button-down. Now that I'm about to come face-to-face with Dasher Valley High's fashionista, I'm regretting that decision.

A million different scenarios on how this reunion could go float around my head. One, she refuses to see me and forces me out of her office. But no, that isn't like Marlee. She will see me and will touch my ankle one too many times just to watch my face scrunch in pain. Marlee will laugh it off like it was just part of the examination and will send me away with painkillers and a broken foot for her amusement. Who cares what's *really* wrong with it?

Or, she may lie and say it's broken just to stick me in a cast for weeks on end when it is only a twist or a sprain.

The ways for her to humiliate me this morning are endless. How can I trust a diagnosis from Satan's Mistress?

"Stella Harper," the nurse calls from the doorway. She looks friendly enough—kind, warm eyes and a soft smile. Lucas helps me up (again, not necessary, but I'll use any excuse to let him touch me at this point because I am weak when it comes to that raspy, southern drawl that's on repeat in my head from earlier), and we make our way toward Room 5. The furthest room in the clinic. Probably because Marlee told her to.

I ask Lucas to head to the room, while the nurse takes my blood pressure, my temperature, and my weight. I've gained some pounds over the past two days. *But that doesn't matter because it's just a number,* I remind myself. I am healthy. I eat a balanced diet (when not in Mississippi). I work out (when my foot isn't a monster of its own).

Just a number. I take a deep breath and crutch my way to Room 5.

I plop down next to Lucas, keeping my eyes forward. I feel his gaze burning holes into the side of my face. "Why do you look like you are fixing to face Calamity Ganon himself?" Lucas asks.

"Facing Marlee Fletcher is scarier than facing Ganon with only three hearts and none of the four gifts from the lower bosses. But you know, I did that successfully. I can do this," I remark, sneaking a side glance at his reaction. His eyes triple in size as his jaw drops open. I peg him with the smuggest expression I can muster. Lucas used to beg me to play video games with him, but I always declined in favor of watching him play. But when I moved to Boston for college, I bought a Nintendo Switch and *Legend of Zelda: Breath of the Wild*. Playing the game made me feel close to Lucas in the moments I broke down and missed him, and to my astonishment, I found I loved the game. My brain thrives on facing problems and finding answers. I'm a puzzle girl and this game was full of puzzles for me to solve.

"I, uh..." His voice trails off as two knocks sound from the door.

Marlee clunks into the office. So, she is one of the doctors who wears heels in the office like in *Grey's Anatomy*. Speaking of, how similar to Addison Montgomery does she look now? They could be sisters. Her smooth auburn red hair falls in soft waves over her left shoulder. Her eyes reflect the piercing cold blue I have come to associate with degradation.

"Oh, my goodness, Stella Harper!" she squeals in her cheer-leader-y voice from high school. I plaster a fake smile on my face the way I always did when she dealt out fake compliments.

"Um, hi, Marlee," I fumble. *We are ten years older, for goodness sake. Get over it, Stella.* "Uh, Dr. Gaines, I should say." Her bright smile widens as she sticks her left hand in my face.

That. Ring. Is. Huge.

"Joseph and I are coming up on one year next week!" Marlee wiggles her fingers. I keep my smile in place as she takes her seat at the computer and continues speaking. "But never mind that. I can't believe you are back in town! Safe to assume it's not a permanent base, correct?" There's the condescending undertone I was waiting to hear.

"Not at all," I respond, squaring my shoulders. "I'm managing Darcy Marshall's bid for the presidency. I'm sure you've heard."

"Oh, I don't watch the news much. Well, good for you Stella! I always knew you'd go off and do great things." *Did you now?* She fiddles with her ring, a smirk pulling at the edge of her lips. "Are you and Lucas back together?"

I feel Lucas stiffen beside me as I feel myself about to word vomit.

"Oh, no. I have a fiancé back in New York City." There it is.

"Really? What's his name? And where's your ring?" *Stupid, stupid Stella.*

"Yeah, his name is Micah. He works on campaigns, too. My ring is being cleaned right now. I didn't have enough time to get it back from Tiffany's before I came back here." Micah does work on campaigns managing social media for me. Half-truths make the best lies, so they say. Tiffany's was a nice touch. She seems to buy it, but why in the world did I say that? "We're getting married on New Year's Day." Lucas makes an awful choking sound beside me. Why couldn't I stop lying while I was ahead? I mentally slap myself right in the forehead.

I glance at Lucas. Every trace of emotion has left his face. He is stone cold. *Uh oh.* Looks like I've put my aching foot into my big, fat mouth.

"Good for you, Stella! Let's look at that ankle. What happened?"

I retrace what has become known as the Suitcase Incident, except this time I tripped over a suitcase at the airport. That's it. No exaggerated stories meant to embarrass each other this go-round.

EIGHT

LUCAS

S he sprained her ankle, and it should heal fully within a few
weeks.

I'm having the darndest time feeling bad for her after that little
announcement, but I help her into my truck anyways.

Then I slam her door before walking around to the driver's side.
I throw myself into the truck, slam my door, and white-knuckle
the wheel, not even bothering to start the vehicle yet.

"You're getting married? In a *month?*" I don't bother to contain
my confusion, hurt, and anger.

"Look, I can explain—"

"You sure as heck better," I bite. I'm trying to maintain my de-
cency here, but knowing the woman sitting beside me in my truck,
who was supposed to marry me on Christmas Eve once upon a
time, is marrying another man in less than a month... You'll have
to forgive my frosty exterior. It could rival the famous snowman
himself.

"Listen, Lucas." The business-like authority in her voice stuns me for a second, and she jumps at the opportunity. "I'm not marrying anyone. I don't know why I said that, but Marlee gets under my skin, and I felt like I needed to prove my worth to her. Which is apparently tied to marriage versus the reality of my career successes." She breathes a sigh of release, closing her eyes and rubbing her temples.

I consider this for a moment, relieved she isn't getting married. But also, I'm wondering why in the world the thought of it made me turn into the Hulk. She has every right to marry who she wants and when she wants. It's been ten years. She has a life, and so do I.

"You know how she treated me in high school," she whispers, her head tilting down. I did. Marlee Fletcher gave Regina George a run for her money. Here's to the countless times Stella made me watch *Mean Girls*.

"So, just to be clear, you're not dating some dude named Micah?" I ask. My heart rate is slowly returning to normal levels.

"No, I'm perfectly single. If I'm married to anything, it's my job." She laughs. "No man wants me. I'm a hot mess right now." The knowledge that she's single threatens to send my heart rate high again.

"Emphasis on the 'hot'," I tease, though I mean every word. Stella's always been beautiful to me. *But you can't go there again,* I remind myself. She punches my arm before turning her reddened face away.

"Why couldn't I just stay?" Her voice is a whisper as if she didn't mean for me to hear the words. She glances back up at me with her icy gray eyes through her eyelashes. Something breaks in me, and I reflect on Jared's words, that I should get to know this version of Stella.

"Maybe we just weren't who we needed to be back then," I say. Her eyes continue to hold my own. I've thought those words many times trying to justify the "why" behind her leaving. *It just wasn't in God's timing,* I'd tell myself. I'm beyond proud of Stella and everything she's accomplished, don't get me wrong. I love seeing her as a powerful, important woman. But she cut me deeply when she left. She stole my future from me in the name of pursuing her own. *Why did she leave?* The question from ten years ago continues to haunt my thoughts.

"Well, ready to go? We have a lot of work to do for the festival, and I need to go to my classroom," I say, breaking the building tension between us and shaking my internal monologue away. No sense in getting into that right now. "We can swing by Honey's first for coffee if you want."

"Oh, um, yeah. Let's go."

"This is your classroom?" Stella's wide eyes roam around the room as she stands with her crutches underneath her, reaching toward me with one hand for her vanilla bean latte. Gracie wasn't at the Café when we stopped by, so we got our drinks to go.

I take in my classroom, trying to see it from her perspective. Biology information posters clutter the walls, with a biology-related meme here and there. The desks are grouped, with a few scattered around the perimeter of the room. A loveseat sits in one corner, with a small rectangular coffee table in front of it. Lights string across the ceiling in a zigzagged fashion, creating a cozy atmosphere.

"Ah," I let out. Her reaction makes sense now. This is not a masculine classroom. "Gracie Jameson."

"There it is." Stella laughs.

"Trust me. There's no way I could have done this. If it was solely up to me, the desks would be in rows, the walls empty, and there'd be no lights." I reflect for a moment. "Though I really enjoy the lights."

I watch Stella as she hobbles on her crutches around my classroom, gently touching the microscope equipment stashed on top of a long cabinet, reading the assignment board that I set up on Friday for Monday, and then eventually plopping down on the mocha suede loveseat. She sits at the end of it while propping her foot up, giving her a full view of my desk.

My chaotic, paper-piled-high-to-heaven desk.

She looks at me, and I just shrug, making my way to sit at my desk.

"Jared's helped me the past five years with the soccer booth, so he knows the ins and outs of it. He was going to run and manage it while I took care of the administrative needs of all the other sports booths." I give Stella the low down. From underneath a pile of papers needing to be graded, I pull out a binder labeled "Frozen

Adventures: DVH Soccer Booth", walk over to Stella, and toss it in her lap.

"Read this. It will tell you what games we do, how we set up, and the vendors we use," I state. I walk back to my desk and sit down, turning on my computer.

As I'm sifting through lists upon lists of athletes, their typical booths, and other information, I hear Stella scoff.

"What?"

"You've done this same booth for the past five years?" she asks incredulously.

"Yeah. And?"

"You've got to change it up." She scooches around so that the binder lies on the coffee table. She pulls the entire table closer to her for easier access as her bad ankle is still propped on the cushion.

Here it goes.

"According to your sales report, the money you've made has gone down incrementally each year." Her eyes follow her finger down a column of numbers. "That's an easy fix. Do something different. Something fresh."

"We already have all the supplies we need to do Frozen Adventures. The kids love it. We aren't changing it. Especially when we only have a week left." That's it. My foot is down.

"Oh, if I'm involved, we're changing it." She meets my eyes before adding with a smirk, "Coach Grady." The way she says "Coach Grady" has me wanting to sit at a student desk with my notebook and pen, hanging on to every word she says. *Yes ma'am. You ask, I'll do.* But *I'm* the teacher here.

"I'll humor you, Miss Harper. What do you have in mind?" I push away from my desk in my rolling chair to get a better view of her, plant both feet on the floor, and lean my forearms on the top of my thighs with my hands clasped together and my head up. This is the dominance pose that shows my class I mean business. "Class in session," I smirk.

She eyes me warily before continuing, but I don't miss the hint of a smile tugging at the right side of her lips.

"First, I need to see what theme everyone else is doing."

I stand up, gesturing to my rolling chair at my desk. "Go on. Look away."

She pushes herself off the loveseat, tucks the crutches under her arms, and clicks my way. While she hobbles over, I pull up the list with all the booths from the sports division of the high school.

Stella sits down and I maneuver around her to hover, making sure she doesn't click on any of the other spreadsheets or programs open on my computer.

"I don't see a Grinch theme, or a Buddy the Elf theme," she notes.

"Taken. The law firm in town does *Elf* and the bank does *How the Grinch Stole Christmas.*"

"*The Nutcracker?*" she asks.

"The dance studio."

"Santa's village?"

"Town Hall." At that, she looks up from the computer and whips around to face me.

"Is everyone still doing the same booths they were ten years ago?" Skepticism plagues her voice.

"Pretty much, yeah," I state matter-of-factly. "That's why we can't change ours."

She laughs, shaking her head.

"No, we can still change it," she says. "But we will have to think outside the box." I pause for a moment, noticing that I implied *our* booth instead of *my* booth. She said *we* instead of *I* or *you*. When did we become a team?

I shake the thought off. "What do you have in mind?"

"I'll need to do a little research and thinking, but I'll have something solidified by tonight."

"If you don't, we are sticking with Frozen Adventure," I warn, still completely unsure of how I let her rope me into this.

"Deal." Stella reaches her hand out to mine, and I take it with a shake. Her hand still fits perfectly in mine. Like it's the missing puzzle piece to my body.

We hold each other's hands a little too long. Our gazes meet, and I slip my hand out of hers.

"Deal."

NINE

STELLA

I sit on the couch taking a break from my campaign work while watching mid-day soap operas with Mama. I haven't seen Lucas in a few days. Between a trip he took with Jared Helms, his best friend, on Sunday and teaching and coaching soccer all week, he's been busy. Gracie has stopped by to visit, but she's been busy as well with her business.

I, on the other hand, have been holed up in the house working on Mr. Marshall's campaign via Zoom with my team, while also making calls and ordering a bunch of stuff for our new booth theme for the festival.

That's right. I pitched an awesome theme Lucas couldn't say no to—Marshmallow Winters. Complete with marshmallow roasting, wintry marshmallow hot chocolate, a snowman made of melted marshmallows, and quite a few marshmallow-related games.

So why do I miss Lucas? I've been busier than ever, yet I find time to miss him. I replay the conversation we had in his truck after the doctor's visit over and over. He practically called me hot. His voice alluded to him joking, but if he once wanted to marry me, then could he still find me attractive? The way I find him attractive? I take a few intentional breaths to cool the heat rising to my cheeks. Why does he make me feel like a schoolgirl with a mega crush?

A gunshot rings out, snapping me out of my Lucas trance.

"Who died?" I ask Mama. She continues to glare at the television.

"They both had a gun, and the camera went off-screen." She throws the pillow her arm was resting on at the TV. "Your eyes were on the show, but where was your mind, dear?"

Lucas comes rushing back into my thoughts, and I know my pale skin is giving me away.

"Lucas Grady," Mama states matter-of-factly. She has always been able to read me like an open book. It's her superpower.

I sigh in response, slouching deeper into the worn leather couch. No use in lying.

"I just, well. It's like one moment he hates my guts, as he rightfully should for the way I left. But then the next he's being all nice and saying things he shouldn't say and letting me change his booth's theme."

"You're single, right, baby?"

"Yes, Mama."

"Lucas is single, too." I was hoping for that, though I never outright asked. But I can't admit that to Mama.

"And?" I question like I'm most certainly not fishing for any more information, though I've put bait on my pole and am throwing it out into the water.

"Maybe it's time to give *Stella and Lucas* a second chance."
Mama raises her brows, but there is no trace of a joke. She still says
our names together like we are a team.

"You've got to be kidding." I laugh, hysteria rising. "I left him. I
did him so wrong. There is no way he would accept me back. And
even if... I have to go back to New York. I'm not staying here. I've
worked too hard in New York, and I am on the precipice of getting
everything I've always wanted. He doesn't want that life. I'm not
even sure if he respects the work I do. He wasn't too happy with
my decision all those years ago."

And therein lies the real issue: Lucas didn't think I could be
successful in politics. He didn't believe in me.

"One, you did us all wrong, honey." My heart shatters and tears
prick in my eyes. Of course, I did them all wrong. I knew I hurt
Lucas. But every time I asked Mama and Stone if they were okay,
they would say yes. Gracie would say yes. They would cheer me
on in my endeavors without hesitancy. Even when my gut, or the
Lord, kept telling me to go home and visit, I couldn't bring myself
to do it.

And I was wrong for that.

"Two, you can ask him to go with you. You never know unless
you ask." Exactly what I didn't do the first time, and I don't know
if I could even do it this time. New York would swallow Lucas
whole and spit him out. He'd hate it.

"Three, I know he respects you. The man is glued to the news.
You know, he gets alerts on his phone in case you're associated with
the headline?" No, I didn't know that. And I'm not sure how to
process that information.

"Lastly, are you sure the life you currently live is the one you've truly wanted?" Yes. *No.* Maybe...

Mama scoots closer to me and wraps me in a hug. "You are forgiven," she whispers against my hair, and I let it all out in her arms. If I'm one hundred percent honest with myself, I don't know if managing campaigns is still what I want to do. I feel like there is something else—something more soul-changing—for me to do. I want to make a difference, but I'm not sure this is how I am supposed to continue doing it. This feeling has been nipping at me for the past year or so. How does Mama see straight through me?

And how did I get so blessed with Marian Harper as my mother?

Mama spends the rest of the day coddling me when I keep telling her it is supposed to be the other way around. I came home to help her out (speaking of, I need to put on my Big Girl Panties and talk to Mama about moving into Heritage Assisted Living Care), not to let her baby my little sprained ankle.

Okay, my humongous, sprained ankle. Thankfully, *Dr. Marlee Fletcher* (I need to stop saying her name like it is cotton candy ice cream—the worst flavor of ice cream) said I could begin walking within a week, given the pain is not overbearing. My progress is ultimately up to me and my pain tolerance.

Though I should wait three more days before I try to walk, I plan to start walking by myself tomorrow. Show them all just how tough, independent, and capable I am.

But until tomorrow, I lift myself off the sunken couch using crutches to go answer the door while Mama finishes her shower.

Standing with the setting sun behind him, Lucas looks like a down-home sip of sweet tea that I could bottle up and save for later. His dirty jeans, cowboy boots, flannel, and tousled mocha hair could be on the cover of a southern smutty romance novel filling the bookshelves in Walmart. The kind you know you shouldn't look inside of, but the cover makes you a little hot if you stare too long.

It's the plate of my favorite kind of cookies, gingerbread cookies, in the design of a gingerbread woman with brown hair and gray eyes, that draws my attention away from the man.

I choke back a gasp as he hands me a cookie with a huge grin painting his face like he is the most brilliant man in the world for bringing these to me.

So what if he is?

I'm still trying to calm the butterflies in my stomach as he maneuvers his way around me to walk straight into the house without me inviting him in. Confidence? Yep. But then I remember he's seen the inside of this house way more than I have in the past ten years and another pang of guilt grips my insides. I should be making him cookies. I should be apologizing until I'm blue in the face. The need to say sorry is overwhelming. Yes, the words he said to me were painful. They took a hit at my pride. But that didn't mean I should have up and left the way I did.

Before I can talk myself out of it, I twirl around...well, I finagle my way in somewhat of a turn as I place my crutch directly on my good foot and howl in pain. Lucas rushes to my side to catch me right as I begin tumbling toward the ground.

I find myself tucked in his arms, hugged close to his chest as if we are on *Dancing with the Stars* executing a perfect dip in a flawless waltz. Is my heart thumping out of my chest because of the almost faceplant, or because Lucas's face is mere inches from my own?

I'd be an idiot to think for one second it was the former.

I feel *something* for Lucas. Even after all these years, he still sets my heart to fluttering when I gaze into his warm eyes.

"I'm sorry." The words tumble out of my mouth, not nearly as flawless as the dance was in my head. He squints his eyes in confusion and begins to speak, but I interrupt him. "I'm sorry I left. I'm sorry I didn't say goodbye."

The silence is deafening, but not as awkward as the fact that I am still cradled in his arms in the perfect pose for a dance-wear company.

"I, umm," I begin to use his broad, stable shoulders to lift myself out of the dip. They feel like solid rocks. So...manly. *Sigh.* He takes the hint and brings me up effortlessly.

"Stell Bells," he says, bringing a hand around to swipe the stray hairs floating in front of my eyes. He tucks them gently behind my ear, his hand lingering across my cheek. My neck. His eyes melt to a smoldering, soft golden burn as he tugs my face closer to his. The tips of our noses touch as his sweet, gingerbread breath washes over me. "I appreciate the apology, and I'm working on trying to forgive you. That's why I brought these cookies over. A white flag of sorts."

Lucas slowly pulls away from me, leaving me in a dazed state of confusion, bliss, and sadness. I watch as he walks to the kitchen counter, picks up a gingerbread *me* cookie, and winks as his lips close around it. How does Lucas Grady eating a gingerbread cookie designed like me make me giddy? What does Taylor Swift say?

Happy, free, confused, and lonely at the same time.

"I'm taking you to see those lights in Juniper Grove you like so much on Friday night," he says with a mouthful of cookie. "Well, if you still like them that is. I know those New York City lights are hard to compete with." Wrong.

"Nothing beats the Juniper Grove lights." A grin sweeps my face. He returns my smile with a breathtaking one of his own. My heart stutters for a moment. He remembers everything about me. He hasn't forgotten a thing.

"It's a date," he says, then catches the very word my heart stopped beating on. "Um, I mean, it's an, uh," he continues to fumble his words. And it's the cutest thing since puppies. "Friends. We can try to be friends again. I've got to go, but I'll text you later with more information. What's your number?" Oh, you clever man. Many single politicians have used that trick on me. I give him my number while shoving down the guilt of having it changed a few weeks after getting to Boston.

"Bye, Luca," I say, his nickname rolling off my tongue like it's been in my everyday vocabulary for the past ten years. I watch him walk out the front door, admiring the way he looks in Wrangler jeans. *Southern men do it best,* the unbidden thought crosses my mind.

"**B**ubba!" I jump up, wincing from the pain shooting up my leg from my ankle. That was a mistake. But my little brother is standing in the doorway! I haven't seen him face to face since he came to New York to visit two years ago. I drop my crutches and throw my arms out for a hug.

"'Sup, Seester?" he asks in his cool-guy attitude, looking at my crutches on the floor. But then a smile breaks across his face and he lifts me in a hug.

"Okay, muscles." I throw my head back laughing. Gosh, I knew I missed him...but I didn't know I missed him *this* much. His laughs melt into mine as he sets me down. I land on the twisted ankle again and bite my lips to keep from wincing. Nothing will ruin this moment.

"All my babies are home," Mama says with heart-eyes. She could very well be the embodiment of the emoji. After picking up my crutches for me, Stone takes a gentler approach with Mama and gives her a soft, but lingering hug. My heart stammers at the scene. How much have I missed these past ten years? How much responsibility did Stone have to take on for himself when I left only three years after Dad passed away? My mood sinks a little, but I crawl out of the muck I've placed myself in.

"How long are you home for?" Stone asks me.

"Until the 27th. I've got to get back to New York to help Mr. Marshall with a string of interviews."

"Well, we better make these nine days count." He winks.

"I plan on it!" Mama and I find a seat on the couch while Stone unloads a few bags from his truck. Both of us are out of commission and useless at the moment. "How's your capstone class coming along?" I search for the remote, finding it shoved in the armrest of the couch.

"It's going," he comments, tossing the bags beside the couch and plopping down on the other side of Mama. We used to sit like this all the time, except Dad would be on the other side of me. I'd nestle into his arm and fall asleep watching whatever movie Stone chose. The memory tugs at my stomach, and I swallow the emotion down. "I regret choosing business sometimes. Those classes can be brutal."

"I think you'll be great at contract negotiation."

"Eh, changed my mind," he says. "I'm thinking I'll open my own business in Juniper Grove after I graduate. We had to develop a business plan for the capstone class, and I like what I did. I think it could work." I watch him speak. He's animated—eyes wide, sparkling, and hands flying with his words.

"Why Juniper Grove?" I ask. "Why not here?"

"What? You're the only one who can move away?" His words and tone take me by surprise, and I sit in stunned silence. "Kidding, Stells." He laughs the comment off, but I can tell there's something more there. I make a mental note to apologize to him later in private. It seems I'm doing that a lot lately.

"Well, son," Mama pipes in. "I'd personally like to hear about this business endeavor of yours." Stone puts an arm around Mama, leans back on the couch, and tells us about his business idea. Turns out, it's more nonprofit work than an actual business, but it grips my heart nonetheless.

"You want to open a community center for kids?" My jaw is slack.

"They need one in Juniper Grove," he says. "I've been working with some kids from their local schools, and they all agree they'd love a place to call theirs. A place where they can find academic help, play games, and just have good, safe fun." Mama sniffles beside me, and I feel a little awestruck myself. Stone has a heart of gold—always has—but he was always saying how he was going to chase the money after college. He wanted the perfect girl, the perfect job, and the perfect life.

"I'm proud of you, son," Mama says, dabbing at her eyes with her shirt collar.

"I second the statement," I say, leaning forward to meet his eyes. "I really am proud of you."

"There's also this girl..." he begins as Mama and I groan in unison. There's the Stone I know all too well. Immediately, I know the girl isn't worth paying attention to because he's telling us. The only girl he's ever committed to was one that we didn't know about until three months in. I think she's the reason for the player of a man sitting here today, but he has never opened up to us.

The rest of the day is spent catching up, annihilating my family in card games, and watching *Elf*. Okay, maybe we watched *Elf* three times. Who's counting?

TEN

LUCAS

Forgiveness is a fickle thing. Once you let it in, other things start to change. You start to change. The hatred drifts away and something else takes over.

It didn't take long to realize I'm happier with Stella Harper than without her. I'd spent so much time lying to myself saying I was better off without her. I took my momma's advice and let her go. I went through all the stages of grief after Stella left me. At first, I denied she was really gone, sure she'd come back and say "gotcha" after pulling the world's worst prank. When I realized she wasn't coming back, anger set in. I wasn't a fun person to be around during those dark days. Then came the bargaining, two years after she left. That's when I bought a ticket to New York and went to bring her back home. The moment I set foot in the city, I bolted back home. I couldn't do it, and that's when I accepted that she was gone. I didn't realize I was still furious with her and had never really left the anger phase until I saw her in that airport. I'd just suppressed it. But now, seeing her, forgiving her...this almost feels like a second chance. Well, at least reconciliation.

I can't afford to think of second chances with Stella Harper. Reconciliation needs to be the goal here.

"You're falling for her again." Jared smirks at me from across my desk.

"I missed her company," I say, shuffling the tests I'd just graded into a pile. "But no, not falling. Just friendly." But even as I say those words, my stomach flips as if to tell me to stop kidding myself. Maybe it's just the chicken from earlier? I'll blame the chicken.

"I don't know what to do with this information," he says slowly. "But please, be careful. She broke your heart once."

"Again, just friends. We were friends before we dated, and we can be friends again. There are too many scars to contend with."

"The biggest lie the world has ever told." Jared chuckles, clapping his hand on my back. "But something is different about her. Maybe second chances are real."

"While I love your wisdom surrounding my love life, I'm here because we need to talk about the festival." I grimace. "I have ten minutes before I need to leave to prep for the soccer game tonight."

"I'll come help," Jared says, and I nod toward his leg. "Right. I can still supervise. Nothing better to do, and I was coming to the game anyway."

"Say no more. Just let me lock these grades away." I stuff the papers into the file cabinet, making a mental note to file them properly tomorrow morning, then lock up. We head slowly toward the truck because hulk-ish Jared on crutches is slower than a turtle.

"Do you have everything pulled out of the basement for the (Not So) Winter Wonderland?" Jared asks, sitting in the passenger seat of my truck.

"Yep. I also found some of Momma and Pop's old things while I was down there."

"Really? What did you find?"

"A bunch of old pictures, tools...and Momma's wedding ring." I pull it out of my wallet to show him.

"I thought you'd lost that?" Jared questions.

"It was tucked away in a box of Christmas decorations somehow. Almost like she was telling me that it was time to pull out the decorations and bring the house to life again." Tears threaten my eyes. I haven't decorated the house in three years. When my parents died in that dreadful car accident on Christmas Eve, I took the decorations down, shoved them in boxes, and stuffed them all into the basement.

Christmas Eve is too hard. Stella and I were supposed to get married on Christmas Eve. Two years later, on Christmas Eve, I saw her kissing some boyfriend of hers on the news. The Christmas Eve after that, I thought I'd found another woman—Jana—who might have filled the void Stella left. But she left me that night, saying I wasn't over my ex after we saw Stella on the news together. Jana had said my mood changed and she'd never seen someone so worked up over "just an ex". Seven years after Stella left, my parents died on Christmas Eve. And now here she is again...with

Christmas Eve slinking closer every second. What will go wrong this time?

It seems my life is marked by crappy Christmas Eves and Stella Harper, I snicker to myself as I fiddle with the ring between my fingers. I'm not sure why I've been carrying it around, but here it is.

I don't know how Momma's wedding ring got in the box of decorations. Those days after the wreck are an absolute blur. The police gave me things that were found at the scene of the wreck. Neighbors and community members dropped off food and rehashed memories of my parents. I was still in denial and shock...waiting for them to come waltzing through the door to wish me a Merry Christmas.

They never came.

"Definitely so. Noelle would have wanted that," Jared says, patting me on the back. "But what do you plan to do with her ring?"

"Put it to good use one day."

"With Stella?" Jared waggles his brows. I glare a pair of razor-sharp daggers his way. He throws his hands up as if to say "or not."

We pull up to the field house and a groan escapes my lips as I take in the condition of the field. The rain did a number on it last night.

"Time to put in some work." Jared laughs at my groan, fumbling his way out of the truck with crutches in hand.

"Need a hand, boys?" A familiar voice calls from behind us.

"Well, I'll be!" I drawl. "Look what the cat dragged in." Stone Harper hugs me with two pats on the back.

"Good to be home." He whistles. "I take it my sister didn't give you too much trouble picking her up from the airport?" Stone's eyes tease as he elbows me in the side.

"She went and twisted her ankle, so it was no issue at all." I laugh, telling him my version of the Suitcase Incident. Stella apparently didn't tell it right because, in her story, she tripped over her bags because she wasn't paying attention—not because she had just seen her very own grown-up Ghost from Christmas Past.

"I figured she'd do something ridiculous." Stone laughs, sliding his hands into his front pockets. "Which is why I waited until she got off the plane to tell her you were picking her up. Turns out I was a smidge too late."

"It was something," I remark. "So how are you doing? How's the last year going?"

"I'll be pursuing a master's after this, so it's not the last year." I raise an eyebrow, and he shakes his head.

"I know, the guy who wanted in and out of school is sticking around a little longer."

"Tell us about it," Jared presses and we make our way to the field while Stone tells us about his plan to build a community center for kids in Juniper Grove. Jared and I exchange glances as Stone speaks, but he is so wrapped up in his plan that he doesn't notice. Something's changed in this man.

"So why are you staying there?" Jared asks.

"You sound like my sister," Stone snickers. We make it to the fieldhouse, and I unlock the door, ignoring the heat-inducing thoughts of *his sister* that are creeping in. We walk into the room.

"Is there a girl?" I don't make eye contact with Stone. One thing I've learned over the years is that he will tell you about a relationship in his own timing. I've only met one girl from his past.

"Oh, I've got plenty. Starting with a date tonight. Sorry, I'll miss your game." His eyebrows jump up and down.

"Who is she?"

"No one you know." He winks, wearing a smirk. I shove the handpump his way. He's avoiding the topic, so I will too.

"Let's get this field ready for game night." I search for the buckets while Jared finds a seat.

"I don't have to tell you that tonight you're facing off with our biggest rival—Harrenburg." The ramped-up boys let out a whoop in anticipation. "We've owned them for the past two years." More cheers. "Let's make tonight round three!"

Their cheers turn into the pregame hype chant as they gather in a huddle beneath the stadium lights. It doesn't take much to get a group of high school boys raring to go. The boys disperse to the sidelines, taking these next five minutes before game time to get mentally focused. I make my way to Harrenburg's coach—Coach Jones—and tonight's referees standing in the middle of the field.

With a shake of hands and a murmur of good luck, we break apart, and I turn to head back to my team.

And wouldn't you know it? Stella is sitting smack dab in the middle of the stands with Jared.

She spots me and a smile lights up her face. She waves her hand timidly, and I give her what I'm positive is classified as a big goofy grin and a head nod of acknowledgment. If I began waving back like a fool at that woman, the people in the box would think I was flagging them down. The parents of my players would start questioning my sanity. Ms. Greene, sitting a few rows back from Stella, would think I finally decided to take her out "on the town" as she once—okay, multiple times—inquired of me.

Yep, it's best to stick to a grin and head nod. However, there's a part of me, and by part, I mean my whole self, that wants to cancel the biggest game of the season, send everyone home, cut the stadium lights off, and drag that beautiful woman onto the field. I would lay down a blanket, pour some sweet tea into a mason jar glass, and we would gaze at the stars all night long, laughing and enjoying each other's company.

Like we used to do in high school.

On this very field.

"Coach!" I vaguely hear Javon's call, but it brings me back to reality. To the boys who need their coach focused on the game at hand and not dreaming about stargazing with his ex-fiancée who left him for no valid reason. A pit of uneasy resentment rises within me. It's funny how that happens even after you've chosen to forgive someone.

"All right, guys. Game time!"

ELEVEN

STELLA

Watching Lucas Grady coach is the hottest thing I've ever seen in my life. Those jogger pants he wears with a black windbreaker shirt tucked in—someone call Dr. Marlee Fletcher because I think I'm going into cardiac arrest. I fan myself despite the chill in the air. He lost his jacket ten minutes into the game, and I lost my will to care that my eyes are cemented to his biceps. I pretend not to notice Jared's wicked grin. I'm surprised he isn't dizzy from the way he's flitting his eyes from me to Lucas over and over.

Jared—an oaf of a man with the softest heart, also has the biggest track record of meddling in all things Stella and Lucas. My brother could rival him, but he left about fifteen minutes before the game because a girl texted him wanting to "chill." Whatever that means to college-aged students these days.

Stella and Lucas. I hate how much I enjoy the sound of that. But I'll have to push it away from my thoughts. Though he said he wants to be friendly again, he has said nothing about anything more. I gave up that chance ten years ago when I took the ring off my finger and sneaked into his house to set it on his nightstand before flying to Boston for college.

Alas, no matter how many shields I throw up against Lucas-centered-thoughts in my mind, memories of all those long, chilly hours we used to spend after his soccer games, lying in the circle of the field and staring up at the stars, kick the shields down like they were paper-made and colored with Crayola. Sometimes we had a midnight picnic, other times it was just us kissing in the name of raising our heart rates to keep warm. I can still feel the haunting touch of his fingers whispering against the nape of my neck and down my back. The shivers devouring my body at the touch of his fingers against my hips. We never went further than kissing, but we didn't need to.

A screaming, shrieking, overly excited mom behind me jolts me back to reality. I'm not sure who started a fire in the stands of the soccer field, but I'm *hot*. My cheeks are flushed with warmth, and I know if I peeled my cardigan off the skin of my arms would be clammy. I quickly refocus my thoughts on the game and... Would you look at that? We're winning! I can only assume it's the shrieking woman's son who just scored the goal.

Lucas does the cutest handshake with the player while Jared stifles a laugh beside me.

"What?" I ask Jared curiously.

"Shh, listen. Behind us."

I slightly incline my head toward the shrieking mom and her friends.

"Bless my heart," she sighs. Like a lover's sigh. "He would be the perfect father for Brandon. Just wait and see, ladies. He's coming around to me."

"Of course that hunky soccer coach is," her friend purrs. Like a freaking cat. "Didn't you see him smile up at you right before the game started?" *Honey, that lopsided grin was for me. Right?*

Another sigh. "Yes, wasn't it the sexiest of smiles?"

"Yes, it was," her friends snicker in agreement.

"I baked him my famous peanut butter cookies. I'm going to give them to him after the game. Men can't resist my cookies," she says. I can hear the sensuality oozing in her voice with every word. She isn't just talking about peanut butter cookies.

Beside me, Jared is visibly shaking with laughter, and when he looks at me with those big eyes, laughter erupts from my lips too.

"Please, for the love of all cookies, tell me she's talking about Ole Coach Johnson and not Lucas," I beg through fits of laughter. Klent Johnson is way past retirement age and was the head coach when Lucas, Jared, and I were in school. Lucas took his spot, but Johnson still coaches as an assistant.

"Mercedes Greene has been practically throwing herself at Lucas for the past two years," Jared says as he adjusts his casted leg in front of him. Apparently, he injured his leg the same night I sprained my ankle. Except I can walk now with only mild pain, and he is sporting a Christmassy red cast. "She's only six years older than him, but you'd think she was a high school girl the way she makes eyes at him. On another note, you should really watch the way the high school girls look at Lucas." He widens his eyes and tugs his lip up in the corner, then sighs into a star-struck gaze. More laughter escapes me at the sight of this giant oaf of a man behaving like a googly-eyed teenager. *God, it feels so good to laugh like this. Thank you for Jared and his unwavering friendship.*

"It's kind of the same way you've been eyeing him all night," Jared states, all traces of laughter erased from his voice. I could deny it, but for as long as I've known Lucas, Jared has known me. "You're an open book, Stells."

"I know," I reply. "I guess there is no use in hiding it. Confession's good for the soul, right? The man still makes me weak in the knees, for lack of a better expression." I watch Lucas on the sideline, running up and down it to keep close to his players. He jumps and claps with wild excitement when they do something good, and he gently corrects them when they make a mistake. What does he never do? Yell and scream. He is so patient with everyone on the field.

"Have you told him that?"

I pause for a beat. Why would Jared want me to tell my ex-fiancé, his best friend, that I'm still in love with him? That I never truly fell out of love with him? That I left after a witless remark he made in a heated argument? Jared should be protecting Lucas from getting his heart ripped out and crushed by me again.

"No, I can't," I say, knowing good and well it's a lie.

"Can't, or won't?" he calls me out.

"Won't. I leave to go back home after the New Year. He will never go with me. I'll break him all over again. I'll break me." That's the rawest thought I have. I won't tell Lucas how I feel, because then I'll just break the two of us when I leave again. I can't do it again.

I won't do it again.

"How was the game, sweetheart?" Mama asks like she's been perched on the front porch swing with a mug of hot cocoa in her hands for the past few hours waiting for me to arrive home. I have no doubt that's exactly the way it happened. Her frail hands are wrapped around the mug and a slight tremble causes the liquid to splash out. I quickly make my way up the steps, ignoring the pain in my ankle at the firmness of my steps, and take the snowman mug out of her hands. With as much grace as a southern woman possesses, she gently wipes her hands down the front of the shirt as if to smooth out nonexistent wrinkles. Her head tilts slightly down, trying to hide the pink flashing across her cheeks.

Mama is not one for embarrassment, but when it comes to not being able to handle her own mug of hot cocoa, I know she's feeling that emotion.

"Oh, it was great," I say, attempting to take her mind from her perceived downfalls. If only she could see herself through my eyes—a warrior of a woman. A woman who could take on every corrupt politician to their face and win. A woman who raised a strong-willed, determined woman such as me. A woman who sacrificed her hopes and dreams for her husband and two children.

"Just great, huh?" She lifts her head back up to its rightful, queenly position. I take a seat on the swing beside her.

"I learned I stand no chance against the soccer moms in a tournament for the love of Coach Lucas Grady." The bewildered look on her face throws me into laughter and she joins in. Her laugh is the sweetest music. How have I not been home in ten years?

"Those women are not to be played with." She snickers. "But I didn't teach you to play. I taught you to win." Oh, okay, Mama. I see you.

"I'm not out to *win* any part of Lucas," I clap back, though my smile gives away all my suppressed intentions. Part of me does want to win him back. And I love a good competition. "I have New York. He has soccer moms."

"You could have soccer moms, though I don't recommend them. Vicious creatures, they are."

"Mama!" I shout through my laughter. My stomach aches from all the laughter tonight. It's the sweetest kind of ache.

"As friends, Stella, as friends. Calm down." She smirks.

"Think they would relocate to New York? We have soccer up there."

"Only one way to find out."

I laugh again for a moment, then settle down. It's time.

"Mama, can we talk about something for a minute?" She is in such a good mood. I pray this is the right moment to bring the assisted living situation up.

"Sure, baby." She pats my hands that are folded in my lap. I unfurl my hands and place one on her leg, letting the warmth of the cozy quilt she's wrapped in warm my hand up. She lifts the blanket and lets me cuddle all the way in.

"How are you *really* doing?" I emphasize the word while holding eye contact in hopes that she will open up to me. To my utter surprise, it works.

"I've been better." She sighs. "I have to admit, it's not easy getting old. Even worse when your own body decides it wants to attack you from the inside out." She chuckles, and I laugh with her, knowing it's her way of coping.

"I know you don't want to, but Mama, I think we should get you set up at Heritage Assisted Living Care." If it was summer, the crickets would be singing a melody in the midst of the silence between us.

"I can't, Stella. I can take care of myself," she finally says with a chill to her voice. I could go on and tell you her reasons—the house she grew up in is right here. She has her friends here. Her life is here. "This house is—"

"I know, I know, Mama." I originally set out to come here, get her into assisted living, and then go back to the city and never return. But now, I don't think returning home would be so bad. "I'll get everything taken care of for you. Or I'll let you make the calls if you want. And I'll come home more to–"

"I do not need you helping me out, Stella," she interrupts. "I am your mother. I help you. That is how this whole giving birth to and raising a child thing works. It doesn't end because you go and grow up on me." Her voice cracks, sadness lacing every word.

"Mama, I don't understand. You know you need help—you said it yourself you're not doing great. Let me help you. I owe you for all you've done for me. Let me take care of you for once by getting you the help you need!" Why is she so stubborn and hard-headed?

"I just, I can't, Stella."

I knew it would be difficult to get her to agree, so I have to let it go for the night. I will lose this battle to win the overall war.

"Okay, Mama," I say, rubbing her back. "Let me at least help you get your mug and blanket inside. You can get yourself." I give her a wink. She smiles and kisses my cheek, letting me know all is forgiven. "Come help me plan Darcy Marshall's campaign trail. I've got countless emails to answer. I've been too distracted." Lucas interacting with his team tonight floats through my recently filed memories. He's fantastic with them. They all seem to truly love him, respect him, and look up to him as their coach. What. A. Man. He'd make a great dad to my future children.

Whoa. Hello, ovaries? I'd like you to tone it down a notch...or five. Thanks.

"That stud will win based on looks alone." Mama makes a satisfied "mmm" sound that jolts me back to the present. That woman could out-flirt Marilyn Monroe.

"I'm counting on it," I sigh, thinking of the million and five things I need to do tonight for his campaign. Where's that original spark I had? The desire to do the work involved with managing campaigns? Of course, I'm still stoked to be the one managing his campaign, but now it feels more like a chore than something I *want* to do. So what do I want to do?

TWELVE

STELLA

The next morning, my stomach wakes me up by twisting and turning. No, I'm not sick. I don't think. It's more of a Lucas-induced sickness if anything. Because today he's taking me to see the Juniper Grove lights in north Mississippi. Which means I'll be in his truck for four hours. And then I'll stroll through a romantic Christmas wonderland with him. With a four-hour drive back.

Boy, oh boy.

I sit up in bed and grab my phone to check the time: six-thirty in the morning. With a sigh, I put my phone down and roll over to bury my face in my pillow.

Nine and a half hours until Lucas shows up at the front door to pick me up.

I force myself up. Typically, I'm out of bed and working by this time. Mississippi time has my body running slower, which I do not mind at all considering how I've been going and going for the past ten years. The hustle is real in the political world.

Grabbing my phone again, I check my emails and send out a few quick replies to the ones I can answer without opening my laptop. But the rest need more attention, so I haul myself out of bed and get dressed for the day.

I think it's time for a solo trip to Honey's to get some work done and to visit Gracie. I've been meaning to spend a little more time with her, but either she's busy working or I am knee-deep in my own work. At least working at Honey's gives me time to sit and talk with her between rushes.

After shrugging on a white slouchy sweater, a trusty pair of black street joggers, and a light scarf, I slip on my favorite pair of olive sneakers (my ankle is much better, but there is still a slight ache). Then I collect my work bag and purse. Before I leave, I write a note letting Mama know where I am in case she needs anything and that I have her car. I hop into her pearl white Camry and head to Honey's Bakery and Café.

"All right, I'm taking my lunch," Gracie says, plopping down in the corner booth opposite me. I look at the time: ten o'clock. I have five and a half hours until Lucas picks me up.

"It's not lunchtime," I mention, looking up from my laptop.

"Perks of being the boss." She blows me an air kiss, and I playfully roll my eyes. "How's the report coming?" I glance over the one page I have written and let the air out of my lungs. Not enough was done in the span of three hours.

"It's going," I say with a huff. I'm way too distracted to focus on this right now. In my defense, I did spend a sole hour responding to emails from my team, different news media, and other politicians that I'm trying to get to endorse Darcy.

But that left two hours to be much further along on this campaign report for Darcy. If only I could get Lucas to stay out of my head for longer than two seconds, that would be great.

"So, do you need a refill or anything?" Gracie's voice catches me. It's unsure, a little wobbly. I meet her eyes, and she looks away and down. I watch as she fiddles with her fingers.

"Gracie, what's up?" I ask, shutting my laptop to show her I'm serious. Though my brain slightly panics as I try to remember when the last time I saved my work was, but I force the thought away to focus on my friend in front of me.

"It's nothing." She shakes her head, plastering a smile on her face. "Don't let me slow you down with your work!" Her voice is several octaves too high.

"You know, I came here to see you," I say, reaching a hand to her across the booth. After a moment, she places her hand in mine. "I was waiting for you to get through the breakfast rush and busied myself with work."

She smiles, genuinely this time.

"So what's up?" I prod again.

"I've just..." She sniffles. "I've missed you. So much."

With that, tears fall from her eyes. I can't stop the ones that form in my own eyes. I get up, slide into the bench beside her, and wrap my arms around her. We sit like that, sobbing onto each other's shoulders, for a hot minute.

"I've missed you, too," I finally say between hiccupped sobs. "And I am so very sorry."

"Sorry?" she asks, pulling away so I can see her face. "For what?"

"For leaving the way I did. For not coming home to see you sooner. For not staying in contact as much as I had intended in the beginning. For everything."

"Stella, you don't have to be sorry. You chased your dream. You answered the call on your life. And you never have to apologize for that." Gracie's hand strokes the back of my head, her fingers tangling in my brown humidified waves.

I take a hand and place it on the back of her head, letting my own fingers tangle in her short, honey-blonde curls. I bring her forehead to mine and whisper, "God, thank you for Gracie Jameson. For her unwavering friendship and love."

We break apart, and she pulls out several napkins from the dispenser on the table. She hands one to me, and I blot my eyes as she wipes hers. Except her mascara isn't leaving her face. I laugh, which catches her attention, and she takes one look at me and laughs too.

"Let me guess, I look like a raccoon?" I chuckle.

"Yep." She nods.

"Well, if I'm a raccoon, you're a raccoon," I say, holding my phone up to take a picture of us. Sure enough, two sets of red, splotchy, raccoon eyes stare back at me.

"If you're a bird, I'm a bird," she replies, and I'm glad she caught my edited reference to the movie we both watched for the first time together and many times after that. Some friendships never end. They are forever, no matter the distance apart.

I wet my napkins using the condensation from my cup of water and blot my eyes. I use my front camera as a mirror and cringe. Why do ladies always look like Medusa in the front camera? I finish fixing my face to an acceptable appearance and wait for Gracie to finish doing the same.

At that moment, the café door opens, and Jared hobbles in on his crutches. I glance at Gracie, remembering Mama mentioning in passing that Jared had a thing for her. I don't miss the red flooding her cheeks, a red that could rival Jared's cast. She checks her face in her camera again.

"You look great," I chime in. "No more raccoon eyes." I nod my head toward Jared, which only deepens her blush.

"Go help him!" I whisper-shout. I watch his face sink as he doesn't notice Gracie at the front counter. The corner booth is situated in a perfect position so we can see everyone coming in, but those coming in can't see us.

"I'm on lunch break," she complains.

"But you're the boss," I remind her. "He looks like his puppy just died." At that, she rolls her eyes. I take the opportunity to shoo her away to talk to Jared.

"Can we hang out later?" she asks as she gets up. I watch as Jared notices her and his smile shines brighter than a kid's on Christmas morning.

"I, uh—" how do I tell her I have a *thing* with Lucas? It's not a date, right? "I need help finding an outfit for a thing tonight." At that, her face lights up. Always the fashionista.

"Totally there," she says, and bounces off toward Jared. I shoot her a text saying to be at the house at two o'clock.

With that, I pack up my work and decide to go ride around the town with my windows down and the sunroof open for a little while.

When I was younger, I hated the fact that Mississippi was so warm during the Christmas season. But now I bask in the beautiful seventy-degree weather.

Because today feels perfect.

I didn't know how much I needed that short, heartfelt conversation with my best friend.

Speaking of best friends, I call Hayden as I drive home because I realize I haven't spoken with her in a couple of days unless it was work-related.

I've got to get better at this long-distance communication thing.

"How're you holding down the fort?" I ask, pulling into the driveway. Hayden's face fills my phone screen. Her black coils are on top of her head, a pencil is tucked behind her ear, and she holds a cup of coffee in her hand.

"Whew, ma'am," she tilts her head to the side, "that accent of yours is back." I cringe, and she laughs.

"Oops, I didn't mean for that to happen." I'll make more of an effort to not let the twang get the best of me.

"The best-laid plans..." Hayden trails off, looking anywhere but at me while scratching the top of her head with her free hand.

"What's going on, Hayden?" She is never shifty like this unless she has something she's repressing. When I first met her, anytime I talked about my parents, she would get like this. Come to find out, she was orphaned as a little girl and went through the foster care system until she was eighteen. She was hesitant to let me in on that part of her life, but eventually, I helped her break down her sky-high barriers. At least with me.

"Darcy Marshall is just insufferable," she finally huffs, slamming her coffee cup on her desk a little too hard. "You manage him so well, but I can't get the man to do anything. It's like if I suggest something, he ardently refuses. But in the next moment, John will suggest the same thing, and Darcy jumps at the idea."

I bite my lip to keep in the laugh that's threatening to spill.

"And he *knows* he's doing it," she continues, "because he will look me dead in the eyes when John walks off. And I swear the corner of his lip ticks up to a sad resemblance of a smirk." My laugh breaks through, and I catch the full force of Hayden Bennet's "you're dead to me" glare.

"Tell me this," I manage to get out. "Did you send our tech guy to suggest whatever you wanted Mr. Marshall to do to see if he would listen? Poor, poor John."

She nods her head shamelessly, a few curls spilling out of her top knot.

"Just come home, Stells," she groans. "I'm sinking without you here." *Home.* Why does it feel a tad weird to call New York City home?

"Hayden Bennet," I lock my gaze with her chocolate brown eyes. "You listen to me. You are very capable of managing Darcy Marshall. Do not cower to him and do not let him push you around. If you want to play with the snakes..."

"Then you have to carry a big weapon," Hayden finishes. "I know, I know. Your little quote is ingrained in my brain."

"As it should be," I nod, satisfied. I hear a vehicle pulling up behind me and see Stone's Ford F-150. "I gotta go, but don't forget who pulls the strings. You are the acting campaign manager onsite while I am away. Use your beauty and brains, love."

We blow each other air kisses before clicking off.

A knock at the car window startles me, even though I just saw Stone riding up behind me.

"'Sup, seester?" He grins, waving a hand.

"Scoot your boot before I hit you with this car door," I holler through the closed window. He takes a few steps back, allowing me to open the car door.

"What are you doing home in the middle of the day?" I ask. He'd been home most evenings, but that's it.

"I've got a date lined up for tonight." He grins. Of course.

"Which girl is it this time?"

"You don't know her." He shrugs, boyish hair falling in front of his eyes.

"Guess we'll see if she can live up to the expectations of Stone Harper." I pat him on the back as I make my way to the front porch swing. He sits down beside me and we sway gently.

"She's pretty, but I'm not sure." He shoves against my arm. I smile, despite wanting to kick his shins. My brother is not a player, well, most of the time. He's just...picky. And he hasn't been the same since the one girl he introduced me to—Lacey Frasier. I only met her once over a Zoom call, but Mama loved her and raved on and on about her. Lacey apparently went to school with him, but since Stone and I are five years apart, I never knew her. I've tried to talk to him about her, but he always shuts down. I can only hope he'll open up when the time is right for him.

"Then why even go out on a date?"

"I'll try any woman once." He winks, and this time I don't refrain from punching his shoulder. "Kidding, kidding," he shouts, rubbing his throttled arm.

"You're never going to find a respectable woman and settle down if you keep finding faults with every girl you take out on a date," I say. "Nobody's perfect, bro."

"'Cept me." He flashes his signature, toothy grin. I don't respond because deep down, I know that he carried the weight of the world on his shoulders after I left for Harvard. He was already becoming the man of the house because of Dad's death. But when I left and Mama got sicker, the responsibility and pressure crashed onto him.

"You're pretty all right," I tease. But then I throw my arm around his broad shoulder and tug him close. Our heads touch as we both gaze out into the front yard. "I lava you."

"I lava you, too."

With those words, I'm transported to watching that cute short film titled "Lava" in theaters before a movie with Stone and Mama. From then on out, it's been our thing.

THIRTEEN

STELLA

"No, yellow is not your color." Gracie snatches the mustard yellow sweater from my hands. "Plus, you're wearing a dress. With boots. No exceptions." *Ugh.* I do NOT miss all the days Gracie dressed me for my dates with Lucas. He thought he was dating Stella Harper—fashion queen. In reality, he was dating the fashion sense of Gracie Jameson—the queen of making average people sparkle like red carpet celebrities.

"But this isn't a date," I protest, though he absolutely said that word. Even if he stuttered around it. No. This is a friendly outing to see the Juniper Grove Lights. An outing for old time's sake. No sir, not a date.

I can't go back there. Nothing has changed. He has a life here, and I have mine in New York.

"It is, but whatever you want to tell your pretty little head." She grabs a dress from my closet and spins around. The cranberry red fabric stares me down, daring me to squeeze my goods in. Mocking me for being two sizes bigger than the first campaign party I attended ten years ago in Jackson, Mississippi. Two weeks before Lucas proposed to me.

Two weeks before I left Mississippi for good.

"I can't squeeze into that dress." I look it over, cringing at the idea of looking like a popped can of biscuits in it. Though I've lost weight since I left home all those years ago, the curves developed and there was no stopping them.

"I'm sure it still fits."

"Gracie, I'll look like the Pillsbury Dough Boy. Besides, it's cold outside tonight, and it'll be colder up north. I'll freeze."

"The sleeves will help keep you warm." I roll my eyes at the idea of lace sleeves keeping me warm as she continues. "You can wear that black leather cropped jacket you wear on television all of the time. Did you bring it?"

I don't even have to look in my suitcase. I brought the jacket—I don't believe in superstitions, but I have won every campaign for my clients while wearing that jacket on Poll Night. "Yes, I have it," I say, slightly disgruntled. I will lose this battle.

"Great," she beams. "Pair it with these stiletto boots from prom."

My mouth drops open.

"Nope. That is not going to happen." I stick my foot out so she can see the still visible bruise encircling my ankle. "My ankle still hurts a little, but if you tell anyone that I will stab you with this stiletto tonight while you sleep. I don't need anyone trying to shove me back on crutches, or heaven-forbid, a black walking boot."

"You won't stab me with anything while you sleep because you're going to be too busy cozying up with Lucas." She feigns a swoon before throwing the shoes down and the dress at me. "Now put this dress on. I'll get those black ankle boots with the small block heels for you." She dips into the small closet.

Ugh. Why is she like this?

But I can't deny I have really, *really* missed her vibrant soul.

Gracie emerges from my closet with the boots in hand while I grimace at the minimal heels. At least these shoes will offer good ankle support.

"In other news, did you hear about Lucas doing a booth at the (Not So) Winter Wonderland tomorrow?" Leave it to Gracie to prod. I know exactly what her next statement will be. "You should help since Jared is incapable at the moment." Ding! Ding! Ding!

"I've already been roped in."

"Oh really?" Surprise laces her voice.

"Yep," I say, popping my "p". "I changed the theme and everything, despite his protests, like the good manager I am."

"Well, that's good! I'm sure he needs all the help he can get to help him get that promotion." *Promotion?*

"What promotion? Principal?" He never mentioned that.

"I'm sure he will tell you tonight," she reassures me. "On your *date.*"

"Okay, quit saying that word with so many implications." I laugh vaguely, still sidetracked by the thought of Lucas as a principal. If that is the promotion.

"Oh, I'm praying for *all* the implications."

"Stop waggling your brows." I lightly shove her. And she waggles them all the way into my bathroom to grab my makeup kit.

Oh, the joys of Gracie Jameson.

Thirty minutes and a face fit for the cover of *Vogue* later, a knock at the door makes my forehead sweat, threatening to take the full-coverage foundation with it.

"Perfecto." Gracie brings her fingers together to her lips in the classic chef's kiss. "Go get your man!"

"He is not my man." I narrow my eyes and flick my gaze to her. I shrug on the black jacket and take one last look in the full-body mirror. My chestnut hair falls in beach waves around my face, reaching down to my chest. The highlights and contours on my face complement my pale skin and make my gray eyes shine like silver. The red dress, surprisingly, fits my curves nicely. It's a little snugger than I remember, but honestly, I look like the woman I always envisioned myself to be.

In my brain, eighteen-year-old me claps her hands in approval and throws herself a celebratory dance party. I'm not sure what we are celebrating, other than looking like a bombshell model right now, but it boosts my confidence.

"Gracie, you're not only an artist in the kitchen but an artist for the human body." I pull her in for a hug, and we only break apart when another knock ricochets through the house.

She shoves me out of the room saying she'll wait upstairs until we are gone to give us privacy, though I adamantly insist she need not do such a thing.

As I'm walking down the stairs, careful not to twist my ankle again or anything, a thought assaults me like a robber in a dark alley.

Why did Lucas knock? He has a key and usually lets himself in. If this is not a date, then why did he knock?

The question still occupies my mind as I reach for the doorknob, taking a breath to settle my nerves. *Get a grip, Stella. This is not a date with your ex-fiancé.*

But when I open the door, Lucas stands there in black dress shoes, delightfully fitted khaki pants, and a black sweater that stretches across his chest. A boyish grin paints his face, and his twinkling eyes draw me in. His dark brown hair styled back—and his beard freshly trimmed—has me wobbly in the knees. This version of Lucas would fit in perfectly in New York City.

I realize too late that I just looked him over and heat floods my face.

"You look beautiful," he whispers, seeming a bit breathless himself. I search for words, but instead, just stand there with my mouth opening and closing like a fish. I can't get over the fact that he traded his faded jeans for khakis, his flannel for a dress sweater, and his boots for dress shoes.

For me.

He chuckles, then pulls out what looks to be a box from Honey's that he's been hiding behind his back with one hand. Because my body still refuses to move to accept the gift, he opens the box himself.

Gingerbread cookies in the shape and colors of Buddy the Elf.

With that, all fears and anxieties rush away from my body, replaced with a sense of home and security.

Because Lucas knows me.

I laugh and take the box, noticing his hand feels clammy as mine brushes against his.

That one touch beckons me to just let go. I'm tired of denying what I feel for this man. We have a past. We know each other. We once loved each other. And he looks mighty fine tonight.

I can let loose for one night, right?

I look him up and down one last time, feeling more confident than ever, and ask, "Are these your teacher clothes? God help those girls in your class."

FOURTEEN

LUCAS

When Stella reaches for the box of cookies, I pray she can't feel how sweaty my hands are. If she can, she doesn't comment on them.

Instead, I'm met with a comment about my wardrobe.

A comment that creates a blush, which heats the sides of my neck, making my hands perspire more. I discreetly wipe them down the sides of my pants as she ogles the gingerbread cookies like she can't wait to devour them.

When her eyes flick back up to meet mine, a grin sweeps my face without my permission. It seems I've had a permanent smile on my face since I finished getting ready for this date—er, outing.

But with the way Stella looks tonight...could this be a date? I might have thrown that word around, but I meant it as *date*. Like, a day and time. But the way she looks...

She should wear that shade of red more often.

"Yes, these are my 'teacher clothes'," I answer, throwing air quotes up. "Except on game days. They let me match the team by wearing our jogger suit."

"Ah, yes. I'm fond of the joggers, too." The words catch me by surprise, but her lips relax into a lazy smile. She's openly flirting with me now?

"Who wins out? Teacher Grady or Coach Grady?" I challenge, testing to see if she will delve out any more compliments. If she can flirt, then so can I.

"Hmm." She looks me up and down. For the third time since I showed up at her doorstep. Meeting my eyes again, she reaches out a hand and places it on my chest. My heartbeat goes triple time. Finally crossing the threshold of the door into the cool December air, she whispers, "I like rugged jeans and flannel Lucas the best."

"In that case, let's run by the house really quick before we leave and I can change," I start walking off toward the truck only to be yanked back by the tug of her hand wrapping around my bicep.

Man, it feels good there. Her touch is almost as good as our banter. I've missed flirting with Stella.

I give in to her pull and turn around to her steel-gray eyes boring into mine. A panicked look flashes across her face.

"I like that Lucas the best, but not that I don't like this one, too." She chokes out in a hurry like she is trying to stop me from snapping my fingers and changing on the spot.

"Well, okay then, Miss Harper." I can't help but look at her hand clutching my bicep. Nor can I help the smirk I feel tugging at my lips.

She jerks her hand away, placing it under her other one, which has been clutching the box of gingerbread cookies.

How long have we been standing near her mama's doorway? Five minutes?

"Ready to go?" She reads my mind.

"Yeah." I hold my arm out for her to take. This isn't supposed to be a date, but the way she looks, the compliments...heck. I put on fresh "teacher clothes" on a Thursday night for her. Maybe this is a *date*. Like a romantic date. "Oh, and I've got one more surprise for you in the truck."

Her eyes blink, and she opens her mouth to say something before I cut her off.

"No, Stella. I won't tell you what it is. Just take my arm and let me walk you to the passenger door."

To my surprise, she takes my arm with a genuine smile.

The venti vanilla bean latte with three espresso shots was a massive success.

I don't think Stella, ridiculously high on caffeine, has talked to me this much since she's been home. It should be annoying, I guess. Given that I like quiet rides and the sound of the road beneath my tires. But I'm loving hearing her stories from New York—stories about a crazy friend named Hayden who pushes

Stella outside of her comfort zone and rather embarrassing stories of mishaps in front of large-scale politicians. I nod, laugh along at her antics and stories, and silently wish I would've been there for them all.

"And then Hayden's face got so red." She covers her mouth with her hands. "Because her last name is Bennett and Darcy is, well, Darcy." I laugh because she is laughing, but I have no idea why that is funny.

"Good one," I lie. She rolls her eyes, shaking her head at me.

"*Pride and Prejudice?*"

"Nope," I smile. "No idea what you're talking about." She shrugs, muttering something that sounds a lot like "men" under her breath.

The truck falls silent, the rumble of the road the only sound. A few minutes pass, and I miss Stella's voice.

"So," I begin, unsure of exactly where this is going. I say the first words entering my brain. "I notice you wear that jacket a lot. On TV, I mean." She continues to look at me incredulously. "To those election party things."

A moment passes as she continues to stare at me. I rack my brain for something else to say. Something that doesn't incriminate me for watching election parties for politicians that have nothing to do with where I live.

"It's my lucky jacket," she finally reveals. "I wear it to every election result night party for my candidates. I haven't lost once while wearing it." A timid smile emerges.

"Superstitious now, aren't we?" I joke, but then I think back to what Jared told me on the phone—*you should get to know this version of Stella.*

Did Stella believe in mystic power voodoo stuff now?

"No, no," she waves the question off. "It's more of a tradition for me to do it now. I have a collection of pictures of me from each campaign election party that I keep. I like the memories," she sighs.

"Do you miss New York?"

"Yeah, a little." I spare a glance from the road to raise my eyebrows at her. She continues, "I miss Hayden and my team. I miss having a wide variety of foods at my fingertips." She wiggles her finger in the air like a sorcerer summoning magic. "But I don't miss the constant go and rush...or the traffic." She sits in thought for a moment. "I forgot what it was like to slow down, breathe, and take time for myself."

"Is your favorite food still Mexican?" At my question, she feigns shock.

"I'm not *that* different now, Luca," I throw my hands up for a moment before grabbing the wheel again. This old truck needs steady guidance.

"Just checking."

"There is this fantastic place called Vida Pura Vida on 9th Avenue that serves the *best* enchiladas." She moans, remembering, throwing her head back. My hands tighten around the wheel as I bite down hard on my tongue. I'm not proud of the way my body reacts to that sound from her lips, but I am only a man.

She must realize what she did because out of the corner of my eye, I notice pink sprawling across her cheeks, matching the sunset outside the truck window. She turns her face toward the passenger window.

We ride in silence a little longer. I'm pleasantly shocked she hasn't attempted to turn on the radio or plug in her phone for Spotify. The past hour and a half talking with her has been better than any song.

"Can we pull over at a rest stop or gas station?" she asks after a few minutes have passed.

"Sure," I respond, checking the Maps app for the next exit. "The next gas station is about twenty minutes away. Can you wait that long?" She nods her head, the pink still lights her cheeks. We spend the rest of the time in awkward, tension-filled silence.

"One hour left to go," I announce after checking the Maps app. It's dark outside now, adding an extra layer of...something...between us. We've talked on and off since we left the gas station, mostly preoccupying ourselves with the snacks we bought.

"We've talked a lot about me," Stella pipes up after taking a sip of her water. "What have you been up to since..." She trails off. "Well, you know."

"After you left." I glance at her. She winces, and I immediately regret saying it. Though we can't tiptoe around the reality of our situation. "I went to Juniper Grove University as planned. I got a degree in secondary education, teaching Biology, with a coaching emphasis. I did my student internship at Dasher Valley High, and I've been teaching and coaching there ever since."

"Is that what you want to do? You always talked about majoring in agricultural science and helping with your family's tea farm."

"The first two years were basics for me. I took a couple of Agricultural classes and found that I didn't really want to study it. I quickly took a liking to Biology and of course, my love of soccer never went away. Playing for college increased my love for the sport. So, I decided to change my major to education to have the best of both worlds." She nods her head.

"The farm wasn't doing too well," I continue, "so after my parents died, I decided to let it grow wild. I couldn't maintain it myself, nor was I willing to sell."

"Do you want to open up the tea farm again one day? Marcy and Lucas Sr. made the best tea." The sound of my parents' names coming out of Stella's mouth twists my stomach. The easiness with which she says their names, and the reverence she holds for them, brings to mind the fact that she never got to say goodbye. Another conversation for another time.

"I don't know, maybe one day. But for now, I'm focusing on becoming the Athletic Director. The position just opened up, and the administration told me the job would be mine if I could show that I could manage more than just my soccer team. So that's why I've been coordinating all of Dasher Valley High's sports teams' booths at the (Not So) Winter Wonderland."

"Ah," she reflects. "That's why Mama shoved me into helping you after Jared broke his leg. You need this to go well."

"Exactly. Though keep in mind I didn't ask her to make you."

"Duh. There is no way you would have asked me to help."

I think about that as I continue to drive. No, I wouldn't have asked her merely five days ago. I was still confused, conflicted, and stunned to see her here. But now? I feel like I've taken a wrecking ball to the walls around us.

Stealing a glance, I catch her looking at me. We both grin and snicker before turning away like we are embarrassed to be caught looking.

"Stella, you can turn music on if you want to," I suggest. Her eyes grow wide.

"Christmas music?" The excitement in her voice sends warmth flooding through my veins.

"You can even play 'The Twelve Days of Christmas.'" I secretly hope she doesn't since I'm playing nice and letting her turn the music on.

With a wicked smile, she hits play.

The most annoying Christmas song ever fills the silence.

FIFTEEN

STELLA

Walking amidst the Juniper Grove lights, I can see why Stone wants to stay here. The antique buildings are quirky and cute. There's an air of comfort and tradition that beckons me to stay. I'll have to come see them in daylight one day. I take a sip of my hot chocolate. Warmth floods my throat as the sweet, creamy chocolate glides its way to my soul. Is that a hint of mint that I taste? Mmm. Deliciousness at its finest.

"I've died and gone to heaven," I whisper, relishing the taste of the sweet hot chocolate against my lips. I don't know if it's nostalgia, but I feel like this hot chocolate is ten times better than ones from New York. Then again, maybe it's just the company I'm with.

"If only I could be that hot chocolate," Lucas says as he turns to look at me with a devil-may-care look.

I spew the drink straight out of my mouth onto the chest of the stunned man in front of me.

Oh. My. Gosh.

His shocked expression makes my insides turn, and I frantically search for words. He blinks repeatedly, reminding me of that blonde man from the famous blinking gif.

"Lucas, I am so sorry," I blurt, covering my mouth like that action could stop the liquid from spewing out in the first place. Napkins. I need napkins. I begin to turn my head every way, avoiding Lucas, and looking for somewhere to get napkins.

"Stella," he says, and I continue to ignore him in my search for napkins. Where are the napkins, people?!

A hand reaches out and lightly wraps around my bicep. Lucas says my name again, and I stop. Why does this little touch make me want so much more? I turn my eyes to meet his as his face melts into an incredulous grin. He starts laughing, and eventually, I join in, letting the stress of the situation float away. I'm secretly thankful the hot liquid didn't get on my dress. I wouldn't have handled it as gracefully as Lucas is right now. Good thing he is wearing black.

My cheeks grow hotter than the remaining hot cocoa in my hand, and I direct my gaze to Lucas, who is standing way too close to me. The words that caused me to spew hot cocoa like I'm a fountain cross my brain again. Did he *really* just imply that he wants to be the drink that is continually touching my lips? Or am I reading way too much into things?

"Stell Bells, you okay?" he asks casually, coming out of his fit of laughter. As if he did not just say those devilish words to me.

"Mhmm," I nod my head fervently. If he's ignoring the comment, then I'm ignoring the comment. My body, however, has different plans. A shudder runs down my spine from his innocent grin, his hand still resting against my bicep. He must mistake my shivers as me being cold because he pulls his hand away and starts to shrug off his hot chocolate-stained jacket. The last thing I need is to be enveloped in his musky scent for the rest of the night. NOPE.

"No, no. I'm okay." I rush the words out. He pauses, then shrugs his jacket back on.

"Whatever you say." Destruction avoided.

But then he walks beside me, wraps one arm around my waist, and begins guiding me forward toward the trashcans to throw away my almost empty cup.

Attempting to ignore the explosion of fire circulating through my veins, I walk forward with his gentle nudge.

"By the way, you look stunning tonight. I remember that dress from the first campaign party you attended. It fit you then, but it *fits* you now," he says, his thumb rubbing circles around my lower back. What kind of monster have I unleashed with my decision to let loose for tonight? He obviously caught on to my flirting and decided he couldn't miss out on the fun. But my word, I'm butter on hot pancakes under his touch right now.

"Oh, you don't have to say that." I shrug off the compliment because it's what I do best. We stop at the trashcan and throw away our now-empty cups. I take another step forward, but his arm drags me back and spins me to face him.

"But I do. Because it's true." His voice drops a few octaves as he whispers in my ear. I can't think clearly with his body pressed against mine. His arms wrap around my waist. After a few moments, Lucas steps away, one arm still around me, and guides me forward. I have to remind my legs to move.

The lights here in Juniper Grove are undoubtedly as beautiful as I remember. The family has added more displays since the last time I was here, and it's all the better for it. But the classic cardboard displays of Charlie Brown, Scooby-Doo, and the Grinch cast of characters are my favorite. The characters are decked out in Christmas outfits, telling the story of the birth of Jesus. Candy canes hang ahead of us on tree limbs, and kids jump up to grab them. We pass under the tree and Lucas reaches up and takes two. He hands one to me.

"Thank you," I say, smiling up at him. He nods and begins unwrapping the plastic from the candy cane. His lips fold around the candy stick, pursed like a gentle kiss. His eyes bore into mine, and I can't will myself to look away. *Dang it, Stella,* I chastise myself. *Stop staring at this man like you want to be that candy cane between his lips! He's not yours to want like this,* I remind myself.

Finding an ounce of willpower, I tuck my head down and begin walking forward on the trail again.

"So, that was a great game you coached last night," I state, trying to tread into the safe waters of mundane conversation.

"Thanks!" Lucas beams at me. "I'm glad you came. It was a surprise, but a good one." I wish he would not act like I made his entire world by showing up to a high school soccer game. It would make it easier to not like him. To leave and go back to New York.

"Of course," I simply say. "I had to come to see what all the fuss was over the 'hunky soccer coach.'" He stares at me wide-eyed, so I quickly tack on, "At least that's what a soccer mom sitting a few rows behind me was gushing about to her friends." He shakes his head and laughs.

"Ms. Greene is at it again, huh?"

"She wants to seduce you with her *cookies.*" I chuckle, recalling the inappropriate use of the word last night.

"She can keep her cookies." Lucas laughs, turning to face me. "I only want you to have my cookies." Now I'm the blinking man gif. What is with this man and his comments tonight? "My *gingerbread* cookies," he emphasizes with another laugh, pulling out a cookie he had wrapped and tucked in his jacket pocket before leaving the truck.

For lack of a better response, I playfully punch his arm before taking the cookie. He catches my arms as I begin to turn away. He spins me so I'm facing him. I gasp, and I'm pretty sure every person here heard it. My head is fuzzy, spinning, as I look into eyes that feel like home.

"I forgot what it was like to have someone in my life who gets me like you do," I whisper against his ear. I'm not sure where the words came from other than the depths of my soul. That and the sugar high I'm riding tonight. His body tightens against me as my breath tickles his neck. We both release the hug, but our bodies are still close together. His peppermint breath washes over me, and I forget where I am. All I want are his familiar, yet foreign, lips crashing into mine. My hands shake at my side. *Lucas, Lucas, Lucas*, his name echoes in my mind. Somewhere, buried deep, *deep* inside of me, I know I shouldn't inch closer. His hand cups my cheek, and, despite the cold, his hand is a little damp from sweat. He wants this just as much as I do. I inch closer. He leans forward. A few more moments and the angels will sing.

"Excuse me, miss," a young child says, pulling at my coat. My eyes fly open, meeting Lucas's hypnotic stare. His hands drop to his side, and I swiftly turn around to address the child. A small part of me wants to curse the day his mother conceived him. But a much larger part is beyond grateful for his little interruption because...I ALMOST KISSED MY EX-FIANCÉ.

"Yes, honey?" I ask, in the sweetest, most southern voice I can muster. I'm still attempting to smash down the naughty elf rising inside me. The elf who wants to lip-lock with Lucas all night under the lights.

"You dropped this." He holds the cookies that I must have dropped when Lucas put me under his mind control. The boy's big, blue, innocent eyes are like water on a hot pan. I'm sizzling out.

"Well, thank you for picking it up for me," I say, in earnest this time. "Here, take this cookie for yourself." I hand him a gingerbread cookie and his face lights up brighter than the lights in the tree above us.

"Thank you, miss," he shouts as he runs off.

"Well, miss," Lucas mocks. I turn around to face him but take a few steps back. "That was sweet of you."

"You know me," I say. "Sweet as pie." I hastily begin walking the trail again, mentally kicking myself for the mistake I almost made. I can't hurt Lucas again. I have to go back to New York. I have responsibilities there, a career. I should have never let myself "loose" for one night because now the lines between Lucas and I are blurrier than words on a page without my glasses. Kissing him now would not be sweet of me. It would just make everything I am feeling more complicated.

But he makes you happy, a small voice inside of me whispers.

I lock that thought up tighter than the ballots on election night.

SIXTEEN

LUCAS

E very nerve ending in my body is activated and at attention. Stella caused that, of course. But now I'm not sure how to come down from the high she put me on.

It doesn't help that she is sitting in my passenger seat with her bare feet on the dashboard in her jaw-dropping dress. When she opened that door, wearing a flowing dress the color of cranberry wine that complemented her body a little too well, my jaw actually dropped.

She's beautiful.

I could imagine waking up to her face every day, kissing her good morning, and making a pot of coffee to deliver to her in bed. I could see little versions of her running around the house, spitting the same sassiness as their mother...

Her screeching voice drags me out of the fantasy I've been concocting in my head. I panic, grabbing the wheel tight and jerking my body upright, checking my surroundings.

"What? What is it?" I hastily question when I see no immediate danger. I glance over in her direction to find her staring at me as if I'd gone crazy. "What's wrong?" She only chuckles.

"I was just singing the song," she states, no trace of humor in her voice. Oh. *Oh.*

"I-I knew that," I choke out. "I was just teasing you." She is not buying what I'm trying to sell. "You know I love your singing."

And with that, a smile bursts across her face and she laughs.

"No, you don't. And that's okay. I'm very aware that I am no Mariah Carey," she pokes fun at herself. I breathe a sigh of relief. "No harm, no foul," she adds. I realize what song she had just been singing along to as the chorus draws near again.

Mariah Carey.

All I Want for Christmas Is You.

Baby.

My stomach twists tighter than a cinnamon knot pretzel from Honey's. It's little things like this—playing a specific song so innocently, when in reality, she pressed play because she wants me to listen to every single word of the song. Words she wants to say but doesn't have the guts to vocalize them to my face.

Stella has a message to send to me through the lyrics of this song. I remember countless silent drives through the countryside. She would play a song, then I would. We had many conversations through lyrics that spoke words we couldn't say aloud. One Christmas, after an argument, she pressed play on this song. When it was over, she asked, "Did you get that?" I shook my head, still a little angry from the fight. She sighed, turned to face me, and said, "When I play this song, remember that I am yours. No matter what we fight and bicker about. No matter how far we drift from each other. This song can bring us back."

Maybe it's naive of me to assume she remembers that promise all those years ago, but the way a smile plays at the corner of her red lips has me thinking she does.

S tella fell asleep shortly after her song, and I drove the remaining two hours in silence, alone with my conflicting thoughts. After we almost kissed at the lights, Stella pulled away from me again. The flirting stopped. Then she played the song in my truck. It's like she can't make up her mind if she wants to flirt with me or just be friends. Or, if she's like me, she can't help herself. When I'm with Stella, especially after tonight, all I want to do is wrap her in my arms and never let her go.

When we finally pull up to her house, I hop out of the truck to get her door. I gently shake her to wake her up, and she does with a sleepy, adorable yawn.

"Thank you for tonight." She blushes, her black boots in one hand and clutch in the other.

"Madam." I pretend to tip my nonexistent hat. That wins me a grin, and I take a picture of it in my mind to save for a rainy day.

When she gets out of the truck, she winces in pain. I notice she isn't putting much weight on her ankle, so I do what any good southern gentleman would do.

I pick the lady up and cradle her in my arms.

And the funny thing is...she doesn't fight me.

She wraps her arms around me, the shoes in her hands digging into my back. But I don't mind. She tucks her head into my chest. *God, I could stay this way forever.* My mind pleads with Him for it to be so.

But we make it up the porch and she asks to be put down, so I gently set her down. She leads me to the porch swing, and we sit in silence. The silence feels like an eternity, but also like just a second has passed. Being with Stella, on this porch, is so familiar that it hurts. I can remember countless days and nights spent cuddling on this very swing, sweet tea in hand, her rambling on about politics while I nodded along and pretended to know what she was talking about. She was always destined for great things. For soul-changing work. I knew it back then, and I still know it today.

And by the stars, I don't think I've ever told her that.

"I've been following your campaigns," I blurt out.

"Oh really?" she mocks, pulling at her jacket. "You are one person in a handful of people who have caught on to me wearing this jacket for every election night."

I shrug, feeling more at ease. She doesn't seem to care that I have TV-stalked her. "You've done a great job for yourself, Stella. I'm so proud of you for what you've accomplished and the politicians you've supported. You always rep for the good ones." Tears form in her eyes, but she blinks them away.

"Thank you, Lucas," she says in barely a whisper. We sit in silence for a few seconds before she speaks again.

"I've been stalking your Instagram." She lets a laugh escape. Immediately, I whip out my phone from my back pocket and pull up Instagram. I scroll for a short time because I only post once in a blue moon.

We're good.

"Had to check for any embarrassing photos that could be used for future blackmail," I tease, looking up from my phone.

"Oh, Luca, I don't need your Instagram for blackmail-worthy photos." She pokes me in the side. She pulls out her phone and navigates around for a minute. With a wide grin, she flips her phone to face me.

And staring back at me is a middle school boy with crooked teeth shown clearly by his carefree, happy smile, hair sticking out like Alfalfa, and his arm wrapped around the shoulders of a petite girl with wavy brown hair. The girl isn't looking at the camera; she is looking at the boy. At me.

"I'm sure you were thinking of how to fix my hair at that moment," I remark.

"Not exactly," Stella whispers, looking away.

"How about wiping the dirt from my face?"

"Nope."

"Then why in the world are you looking at me like that in this picture, Stell Bells?" I'm fishing for compliments, and I'm not even ashamed.

"Oh, I was just thinking of what you would have done if I would have leaned over a few inches and planted a kiss right on your dirty cheek," she says, no trace of humor in her voice. Her gray eyes bore into mine, and my body decides it's a statue. Without breaking her eye contact, she leans across the swing and kisses me on the cheek. I feel the heat rising to my cheeks as she backs away. Her kiss haunts me like phantom pains. I can feel her soft lips pressing against my skin over and over. I want more.

I'll have to find a way to earn more cheek kisses.

"So, I guess you should get inside."

"I guess I should," she says. Neither of us moves.

"Goodnight, Luca," her eyes sparkle under the porch light.

"Night, Stell Bells."

Except she still doesn't go inside, and I don't walk down the front porch stairs. I want to stay a little longer. Against my better judgment, I want to be with Stella Harper again. Admitting it feels right. It could be because it's midnight, but mostly, it's the blatant realization that in the ten years Stella and I were apart, no other woman has made me feel the way she makes me feel. No other woman has come close to her. Thankfully, I have the perfect excuse to stay a little longer.

We need to get the Christmas decorations up here at the Harper House.

"This house needs decorating," I say. "If you're up for it."

"I think you're right," she whispers. "I'll throw a pot of cider on."

SEVENTEEN

STELLA

After checking on Mama, who is sound asleep with her loud fan on, I take a pot of cider Mama made not too long ago out of the fridge and heat it up on the stove. As it warms, the aroma fills the house, creating a cozy atmosphere. I run upstairs to change out of the dress and into leggings and my white sweater.

By the time I make it back to the living room, Lucas had pulled the decorations out of the storage room and set the tree up. I stop, leaning against the opposite wall from the tree, holding two warm cups of cider in my hands. I watch as he unpacks the angel. He notices me and grins, then proceeds with straightening the angel's dress out.

"Don't spit your cider on me this go-round," Lucas teases. Heat floods my face with embarrassment, but thankfully, he's not looking my way. I take the opportunity to get lost in the sight of him.

This is what being high feels like. I'm sure of it. I've never done drugs, not even a taste or a puff. But Lucas Grady puts me in the clouds. His smirk, the boyish twinkle in his eyes, the way his muscles bulge as he places the angel at the top of the Christmas tree....

"Stella? What's your answer?" Lucas saying my name snaps me out of my haze. And I realize I've probably been ogling him for a hot minute now.

I clear my throat.

"Yes?" I say an answer like a question, hoping I answered right to whatever he was apparently asking me. He chuckles under his breath.

"Good to know." He shakes his head. What is good to know? What did he ask me? I can't ask because it'll be a dead giveaway that I was watching his body instead of listening to his words.

Trying to distract myself from pondering on it too much, I notice the angel is crooked at the top of the tree. I reach up to fix it.

He's behind me suddenly. If I turn around, I will be staring at his chest. His solid, warm, inviting chest...

Snap out of it you big twit. Nothing good happens after midnight.

I feel his body lean against mine, a ghost of the past coming back to taunt me. I become as still as Frosty before he was brought to life. Lucas's large hand slides up my lifted arm slower than Congress moves until he reaches the golden angel at the top of the tree. He tilts it just enough to correct the error. His hand lingers on the angel while his body presses tighter against me. The needles of the tree pinch through my sweater and into my skin, somehow making this moment hotter.

"I thought you told me the angel looked good," he whispers in my ear using a low rasped tone. His hot breath washes across the back of my neck, sending needles pricking down my spine like the ones physically pressing into me. It's like my body is covered in prickly pine needles now.

"I, er—" What are words? The girl who has given a million speeches can't think of a single word. She also can't seem to move.

"It's okay. Better now?" His voice is raspy like he has been a chain smoker his entire life. Though I know for a fact Lucas has never even tried a cigarette. At least when I knew him...

That thought alone rips me from the hypnotized trance I was in. I finagle my way out of his body shield and look at the tree from the middle of the room. In a nice, safe, Lucas-free zone.

"Yes, lovely. Perfect." The words are rushed, my brain still reeling from his nearness.

He walks over to stand beside me. Close enough that I feel the heat radiating from his body, but not close enough that we're touching. *Leave room for Jesus,* my mama's words float into my head.

"Yes, it is perfect," he says, but he's not looking at the tree. He is looking down at me. There goes my face acting on its own accord again. Getting all red for its own convenience.

"Okay!" My voice is too high and unnatural. "Let's get the ornaments on!" *Tone it down, Stella.* I grab the green box filled with ornaments and drag it to the tree. Opening it up, my heart skips a beat remembering many, many Christmases ago when Lucas and I were in this very room. Doing this very thing. With the very same ornaments. Mama hasn't changed a single ornament. I look through the box looking for something non-familiar. But I can't find anything.

"She likes tradition," Lucas says, peering into the box over my shoulder. His nearness startles me again. Why does he keep coming up behind me like that?!

"Mhmm." I nod my head. "Well, let's get busy." I reach in, grabbing a few of the ornaments I made during my childhood—a star with glitter (though most of the glitter has fallen off), a popsicle stick cross painted red with green hearts, and a snowflake made of papier mâché. I find spots for these on the backside of the tree, while Lucas starts putting the red and green glitter ornaments on the front.

"Remember these?" Lucas asks me, holding up Mickey and Minnie ornaments that we hand-painted our second Christmas together. My mind flies back to that night, remembering the laughs, the music, the kisses.

"I remember." A smile spreads across my face without permission. He returns the smile and gives me the Minnie ornament to put on the tree. Naturally, the only place Minnie belongs is right next to Mickey, so I slide closer to Lucas and wait for him to place his Mickey ornament. As he puts his on, I bring mine up to hang right beside his. Our fingers brush as he pulls back, and I put Minnie on the tree. Again, he lingers more than he should. But this time, I don't pull away either. Instead, I turn my head and meet his golden, caramel eyes. So many unsaid words are laced into that one-finger touch. What a sight we must be. Two people getting worked up by letting our fingers touch together on a Christmas tree...

We both pull away at the same time and look away from each other. I can't do this. I think I might combust like a dying star.

We finish the tree quickly with Michael Bublé singing softly in the background. Yes, we had our own mini concert when "It's Beginning to Look A Lot Like Christmas" came on. And that's when Mama hobbled into the room with a fierce glare in her cold eyes. We turned the music down and our silent giggles took the place of Bublé.

"Next time you two are going to be up at two o'clock in the morning, making my house smell and look like Christmas," she continues to glare, "invite me to the party." With that, her face breaks into a grin, and Lucas and I sigh in relief at the same time.

I don't know what was better: Singing with him or sharing silent, knowing looks like we were teenagers sneaking around again.

But whatever it was, I realized something tonight.

I still want to do soul-changing work.

But the draw of returning to New York is fading for me.

The draw of Lucas is growing with every second that ticks by.

EIGHTEEN

LUCAS

I take a sip of my second cup of coffee for the day, leaning against my truck. Unlike Stella, I usually drink one cup a day. But after the late night and the embedded early morning teacher alarm clock in my body, I need an extra cup here at noon to get through today. It was hard to sleep when I got home because Stella was on my mind. Last night felt so right. It felt like old times. We were Lucas and Stella again. Two invincible people who could solve world hunger as long as we were together. I've almost kissed her twice now, not to mention all the times I have thought about it since she's been home. But I'm waiting. I don't want to kiss her until I know it's what she wants. Until I know her heart is matched with mine again.

"Car is loaded down!" Stella's voice rings out, and I wonder if she knows I was just thinking about her. She definitely caught me looking. And man, she looks good in her business outfit—black pencil skirt, a red sweater tucked in with a white collar showing underneath, and the black boots that she wore to the lights in

Juniper Grove. Her hair is in a knot at the nape of her neck, inviting me to touch it. The woman I've come to know over television is standing right in front of me, and I find I love this side of her. All business, poise, and just plain hot.

"Almost done with mine," I holler in response, turning my attention back to the task at hand. We're finishing packing all the booth supplies into her mom's car and my truck.

"Need a hand?" I feel her presence behind me as I lean over the truck tying down the wooden arches.

I turn around to find Stella face to face with me. Her gray eyes are level with my lips, though they look up at me with a myriad of emotions. I have the sudden urge to wrap my arms around her and pull her against my chest.

I resist, opting to flash her a smile and watch as a pink blush colors her cheeks and her eyes flick to my lips. Ever so slightly, she bites down on the edge of her bottom lip, causing a blizzard of butterflies in my stomach. Does she feel the same way I do? Does she want to kiss me?

Because the way she is looking at my lips has me letting go of my former plan to wait to put my lips on hers.

"Nah, I'm done," I say, leaning a little closer to her. She stands still as a statue.

"Okay," she chokes out, breathlessly.

"Okay," I whisper back, leaning in again, centimeter by centimeter.

Something flashes in her eyes, and she shakes her head.

"Well, let's get going then!" Her voice is a little too high. I take a step back. A little disappointed, but completely understanding,

I agree with her that we should go. She walks quickly to the car, slides in, and cranks it up.

I climb into my truck and follow her lead to the festival.

Make that three almost-kisses.

With my windows rolled down, I can hear the music before I see the park. "Carol of the Bells" rings out over the loudspeakers while people bustle around setting up booths. As we unload the decorations at our spot, we are assaulted with the smells of fresh cookies, apple cider, and pies.

"Hey, Coach! Where d'ya want us?" Brandon asks with Javon, Cody, and Devin trailing behind him. The boys are wearing their white jersey tops to match our Marshmallow Winters theme. I'm impressed that my four seniors are here, ten minutes early.

"Look who's showing great leadership today." I nod in approval and the boys' chests swell a bit. I like to take every opportunity to affirm a hard work ethic and respectful manners. "Help me get this arch put up for the entrance to the booth." The boys immediately take sides and hoist the wooden arch up. "Why don't y'all get started on decorating the interior."

"Uh, Coach. The girls usually do that part," Javon says, a look of panic on his face at the idea of decorating.

"Guess we got here just in time," Madison, senior and captain of the girls' soccer team, calls out. The entirety of the team stands behind her like a posse. They wear their white jersey tops as well, along with white bows pulling their hair back. I spot Brandon laughing nervously, and then I glance at Stella, who is pretending to unload decorations but is actually watching Brandon's reaction to Madison too. Jared and I have an ongoing bet—I think Brandon will man up and ask Madison out before the end of the school year, but Jared thinks he won't, and Madison will make the move. I'll have to let Stella in on it and get her to encourage Brandon in my favor. Madison continues, "We've got this, boys."

"All right," I drawl, taking attention away from Brandon's ever-reddening face. "Let's get the rest of the stuff from the trucks so I can walk around to check on the other booths."

After unloading all we need for our booth, I pull Stella to the side.

"Can you monitor the set-up while I walk around and check on the rest of the sports teams?" I ask her.

"Of course," she says, "I was born to run things."

"I have no doubt about that," I laugh. Her face falls slightly, and I have no idea why. "Everything okay, Stell Bells?"

"Yes, yes," she says hastily. "Now go check on the booths so you can get that Athletic Director's position!" She shoves me toward my clipboard and binder sitting on the hot chocolate table.

"Okay, ma'am." I throw my hands up, surrendering to her. I pick up my stuff from the table and take one last look at Stella before I leave. She has already busied herself helping the girls' team set up the marshmallow snowman. The boys are busying themselves by throwing marshmallows.

"Greene, get your team in check," I command Brandon, using his last name to show I mean business. He stiffens and begins to halt the marshmallow assault. I walk away, semi-confident that they all have this in control.

NINETEEN

STELLA

B arking orders is one of my favorite things to do.

"Madison and Brandon," I begin, choosing those two solely because of the way they keep looking at each other with googly eyes. "Set up the Marshmallow Toss." I see mischief pass through Madison's eyes. "And don't start the game until kids arrive," I add for good measure.

I shake my hands out, examining the scene unfolding around me. White drapes cling around the wooden arch, melting into the white ease-up tent behind it. The hot chocolate table stands inside the tent, covered with a toasted brown tablecloth to resemble a toasted marshmallow. Mama should be here in the next hour with the hot chocolate and the fixings. The boys are helping the girls string up white and silver papier-mâché to the top of the tent to create a snow effect.

"How's it going?" a bubbly voice calls from behind me. I turn around to find Gracie walking up to me with a coffee cup in each hand. She holds one out to me.

"Bless you," I say, reaching out to take the to-go cup. I take a sip and sigh as the delicious vanilla flavor leaps over my tongue.

"You never called me after your date," Gracie prompts. I begin to remind her that it wasn't a date, but I'm not so sure anymore. I gesture at her to follow me as we go sit down on a couple of chairs just outside the ease-up.

"When we got home at like twelve in the morning, we decided to decorate Mama's house." I watch her blue eyes widen.

"Details!" She shakes my arm, and I hold the cup of coffee out to keep it from splashing on me through the drink hole. I motion at her to quiet down because the entirety of Lucas's team is around us. She mouths an apology while her face obviously says she's not sorry.

I take another sip of my coffee.

"Something has changed between us," I say, looking for the right words. "We almost kissed last night. And then again this morning before we came here." Her eyes bulge out of their sockets.

"He stayed with you last night?"

"No!" I exclaim. "No, he went home after we finished decorating. I met him at his house to help bring the festival stuff over and we had a moment."

"Please go on about this 'moment,' and the almost-kiss last night. And I mean I want aaallll the juicy details." She winks.

"There's nothing much to it, honestly. We just got a little too close to each other while under romantic Christmas lights." I shrug. Gracie rolls her eyes.

"Sure, blame wanting to kiss the very hot man on Christmas," she chuckles. "What about earlier today? Were you under the mistletoe or something?"

"No, again..." I trail off, remembering the heat of his body against mine, contrasting the wintry chill in the air today. The way his lips slightly parted, inviting me in. The smell of sunshine and coffee rolling off his skin.

"You got a little bit of," Gracie gestures to the corner of her mouth, "drool there."

I let out a very unladylike grunt of frustration and Gracie busts at the seams.

"You got it bad, Stells."

Before Lucas left to check on the other teams and booths, he told me he had no doubt that I was born to run things. I knew it was a compliment, but my thoughts flew back to ten years ago when he told me that my career choice was just a silly dream. If he knew I was born to run things, then why didn't he tell me that ten years ago? Did it really take him this long to figure out I had a knack—a gift—in the realm of managing and organizing? And that I wanted to use it for good and for change?

"So, what's stopping you?" Gracie asks in the silence.

"Do you know why I left?"

"You needed to pursue your dream while the offer was there," she says, repeating back the words I used as an excuse to leave.

"Well, yes," I begin, "but there is more to it." I tell Gracie about my anxiety attack after Lucas proposed to me. I tell her of my past conflicting feelings about getting married at eighteen. I tell her about getting the Harvard letter in the mail and how it felt like a sign from God to go. And then I tell her about Lucas's reaction when I told him.

She thinks for a minute, a crease interrupting the space between her eyebrows.

"You left because an eighteen-year-old Lucas was hot mad that you wanted to go to Harvard right after you accepted his marriage proposal?" When you put it that way...

"I was eighteen, too, Gracie. I had the offer of my dreams in my hands. I wanted to make it work, but then he went and said those words that boiled my blood." I take a breath, willing her to understand my side. "The words every other person throughout school used to tell me. That it was a silly dream. That a small-town girl from Mississippi could never make something of herself."

"I get it, Stella, I really do." Gracie puts a hand over my own. I clutch her hand, trying to forbid the tears pricking at my eyes from falling. "But maybe you being here now means something. A second chance, perhaps? It is Christmas, after all. Anything can happen."

"I know it means something," I state. "I've been trying to fight it, but dear heavens, I missed Lucas Grady." With the admission, a tear escapes, sliding down my cheek. "I got over his words a long time ago. It was silly, immature, and foolish for me to leave the way I did. But when I came to that realization, I was too embarrassed to come back or reach out. Too much time had already passed."

"Miss Stella!" a voice calls me from somewhere inside the tent.

Wiping the tear away, I call back, "Out here!"

Javon and Brandon approach, Madison and another girl whose name I can't remember flanking their sides.

"You good?" Javon asks, apparently noticing the buildup of water around my eyelids.

"Good as pie," I respond, blinking the liquid away. "What do you need?"

"*Someone,*" he shoots daggers in the direction of Madison, "decided it would be a good idea to put glitter on the outside of the hanging marshmallow lights and the glitter spilled all over the real marshmallows for the Chubby Bunny challenge."

"You're the one who shoved me while I was applying the glitter," Madison fires back.

Javon opens his mouth to say something else, but I interrupt.

"Hey, it's not a big deal," I tell them both. "I'm not a huge fan of that game anyways because of how dangerous it can be, so why don't we hang up the glitter-fied marshmallows as well? We can also make marshmallow trees out of them for more decoration."

They stare each other down a moment longer before agreeing to my suggestion.

"You're good at this," Brandon remarks as the others walk out. "Coach is a lucky man."

"Oh! We're not together." But even as I say the words, my soul yearns for him.

"Hmm," he shrugs. "That's too bad." Then he turns and walks back into the tent.

"I want my future babies to skip the teen years," Gracie scoffs. I couldn't agree more.

"Where do you want the hot chocolate?" Mama calls out while walking up to our booth, holding the crockpot of chocolatey goodness. I meet her and take it from her hands, knowing it must be hurting her, and bring it inside the tent to set it on the table. "Johnny has the fixings." As if summoned, Brother Johnny Howell appears in the tent with several grocery bags.

"I tried to bring the crockpot, but she wouldn't let me," he says, setting the bags on the table.

"That's Mama for you," I huff. Mama smiles up at him with a twinkle in her eyes. Maybe I could approach her again about moving into an assisted living home tonight since she seems to be in a rather joyful mood.

"Oh, hush, you two." She swats the air. "I'm perfectly capable."

"That you are," Brother Johnny croons, his gaze burning into Mama's own. I look away, not wanting to watch Mama flirt with another man. I know she loves Dad. She always will. But it's hard to watch her try and move on.

"All the booths are set up and looking good," I hear Lucas's voice outside the ease-up tent. My body responds, wanting to run out to meet him. I will my feet to stay still.

He goes on talking to his team and the girls' team, praising their work and complimenting their designs and decorations. My heart feels like it might burst.

I hear someone tell him to go see the inside, and my heart begins to beat triple time.

A few students trickle in, waving at me with huge smiles. Then Lucas appears behind them, his gaze roving around the booth until it settles on me.

I throw my hands out as if to say, "What do you think?"

Instead of answering, he moves toward me and picks me up in a hug. His trimmed beard rubs against my cheek as he whispers against my ear, "Thank you so much, Stella."

Lucas sets me down too soon.

"It was nothing," I reply in a daze.

"Seriously. I couldn't have done this without you and your fresh ideas."

I shrug to repeat my previous statement, not trusting words at this point. The smile on his face has me weak in the knees. It's a smile that screams joy and contentment. Like this is indeed a very merry Christmas for him.

At this point, a few kids trickle into the booth asking for hot chocolate and to play the Marshmallow Toss game.

"Game on," Brandon and Madison say at the same time. They meet each other's gazes and blush. I glance at Lucas who is still smiling at me like I hung the moon.

We break into our previously assigned jobs and the (Not So) Winter Wonderland is underway.

Mama takes a place at the hot chocolate table beside me, and we busy ourselves serving the kids and adults that come through. About thirty minutes in, we have a slight lull, and I jump at the opportunity to talk with Mama.

"Brother Johnny, huh," I start. "How long has this been going on?"

"Oh, he's been helping me out here and there since his wife died a few years ago. We found solace in each other's company."

"So, is this a thing?" My heart clenches and my hands tremble slightly. I want her to be happy, I do. I guess no amount of time completely takes the pain of losing a parent away.

"It is," she says, going starry-eyed. "I think he may propose soon." I gasp, letting the words sink in.

"Wow, Mama." I search for words. She takes my hands and places them snuggly in her own, her smile settling my spirit. "This is wonderful news." And I genuinely mean it. Her happiness is radiant.

"Guess this means you can't stick me in a home," she says as she elbows me.

"I was going to pester you about it again tonight." I shake my head. "But if Brother Johnny indeed proposes to you, then I guess you're in pretty holy hands." Mama rolls her eyes at my bad joke, though we both laugh.

"Holy, hot hands." She winks, shimmying her shoulders. I rip my hands from hers in mock disgust. Crazy, wonderful woman.

TWENTY

LUCAS

"Slip out with me," I whisper against Stella's ear as she serves hot chocolate. I see the drink tremble in her hands and a wave of satisfaction washes over me. She thanks the person for coming and donating to the soccer team, then follows me out of the tent. I nod to Jared, who is sitting just outside the tent next to Gracie. He doesn't even acknowledge me, and the stupid grin on his face tells me all I need to know.

"Where are we going?" She rubs her arms. I slip off my brown coat and offer it to her. To my surprise, she takes it. I watch her slip her arms through and...did she sniff it?

"Let's walk around and enjoy the festival. The team has our booth running smoothly."

"Okay," she agrees with a smile. Stella looks around, taking in the atmosphere. Every inch of Dasher Valley Park is decked out in all things Christmas. As we pass booth after booth, new smells assault us—cookies, pies, and even jambalaya. My stomach growls.

"Oh! Can we stop and get Pineapple Jambalaya?" Stella asks. "I haven't had it in forever!"

"You read my mind," I tease. I ask Mrs. Phyllis for two bowls of the spiced rice, pineapple, sausage, and chicken mixture.

"Where are your proceeds going this year?" I ask Mrs. Phyllis, who chooses a new charity every year to donate the money she makes from the festival to.

"Hannah's Hope," she replies with a smile. "It's a group home opening in the city."

"How sweet," Stella replies, taking her bowl from Mrs. Phyllis.

"Stella?" the elderly lady questions.

"It's me," Stella waves inconspicuously.

"Come here, dear," she says as she comes out from behind the table of her booth. She embraces Stella before stepping back. "Let me get a look at you."

"How have you been, Mrs. Phyllis?" Stella asks.

"I've been fine," she says. "I'm so happy to see you back with our Lucas." I cringe, trying to make myself invisible in the background. But Stella finds my eyes and I see a battle raging within them.

"We're not together," I butt in abruptly, trying to calm the fight in Stella's eyes. I knew she didn't want to be with me, but a part of me was hoping she had changed her mind. Apparently not.

"Too bad," Mrs. Phyllis says, and Stella stifles a laugh. Really? It's funny now?

I thank Mrs. Phyllis and go find a seat on the nearest bench underneath a streetlight. I don't check to see if Stella follows, but as soon as I sit down, she takes a seat beside me on the opposite end of the bench.

We sit and eat in silence for what seems like an eternity until Stella asks me a question that befuddles me.

"Why did you tell me my career choice was a silly dream?" What in the world is this woman talking about? Her eyes bore into mine, waiting for an answer.

"Stella, I have no idea what you're talkin' about."

Her legs bounce up and down. She looks down at her almost-empty bowl of jambalaya, then rolls her shoulders back, sitting up straight.

"When I came to you the day after we got engaged, I showed you my acceptance letter to Harvard..." she trails off, worrying her bottom lip. I rack my memories for where this is headed. Nothing. I was angry, upset, and confused when she told me she wanted to take the offer at Harvard. I mean, we had just gotten engaged. She resumes, "You told me that it was a silly dream."

"I said and thought a lot in that moment that I shouldn't have. Things I didn't mean," I gently say, still trying to recall that phrase. That whole scene is muddy water in my head.

She takes a few breaths, then nods, "I know."

I set my empty bowl on the ground beside the bench and reach a hand out to her. An offer, not a demand.

She sets her bowl down and takes my hand.

I scoot closer to her, turning my body toward her. She turns into me. I rest my free arm around her shoulder, and she tilts her head down.

Releasing her hand, I caress her chin, tilting her head back up so that her icy gray eyes see me. See me, please. *Let her see me,* I plead silently with God.

"Stella Harper," I begin, bringing my hand back down to hold hers, "there is not a single moment that I've not been immensely proud of you and the things you've accomplished. I always knew you'd do great things. You getting into Harvard didn't take me by surprise." I pause, letting my words sink in. Then I admit the one thing I'd stuffed down since the moment she ever agreed to date me. "You were always too good for me. I was holding you back. And I hated myself for selfishly wanting you to stay here and build a life with me. You were always destined for more." Tears pool in her eyes, and I feel mine misting up.

She sits there, mouth agape. The tears begin slipping from her eyes, and I reach out a hand, my palm cupping her cheek to wipe the tears away with my thumb.

"You ridiculous, incredible man!" A disbelieving laugh escapes Stella as her voice grows louder with each word. I draw my hand back. "I could beat you!" She throws her head back in an almost maniacal laugh, covering her eyes with her hands. After a moment, she places her hands on her thighs, rubbing them against her black pencil skirt. "If you and your stubbornness could have just admitted that nonsense to me ten years ago, I might have my career and we might have been married with babies!"

I scoff, "How would we have made that work?"

"It's called technology and patience, you fool." She shakes her head, still laughing like she hasn't laughed in years. She pulls at the bun on top of her head, chestnut brown hair falling in waves. I let her release whatever emotions are overwhelming her. When I catch someone staring as they walk by us, I shoot them an "I'll-kill-you-if-you-say-something" glare. Her laughter slowly recedes, and she gasps for breath.

Immediately, I pull her body backward into mine, wrapping my arms around her from behind. Her hands fold over mine, her firm grip driving her nails biting into the skin on my hands. I clench her closer to me.

"Breathe, Stella." I guide her with my own deep breaths. The rhythm of our breaths merge into one, chests rising and falling—in, out. A few minutes later, Stella is calm, and she relaxes her head in the spot between my head and shoulders.

"I'm sorry," she whispers. I squeeze her impossibly tighter.

"You have nothin' to be sorry for," I say as I fiddle with her hair.

"I never wanted to leave you," she says. I let the admission wash over me, her words igniting a flame in my veins.

I believe her.

"You want to go walk around some more before they start closing this thing down?" I ask. She pulls free of my arms and sits up to face me. A smile tugs at the corner of her soft, pink lips. The streetlight glows above us, making this heavenly woman in front of me shine.

"Can we just sit here a little longer?"

"Anything you want, Stell Bells." Stella slides close, takes my hand, and rests her head on top of my shoulder.

I am the luckiest man in the world right now.

TWENTY-ONE

STELLA

After getting off the phone with Mr. Marshall for an impromptu meeting regarding his campaign route, I snuggle into my warm childhood bed.

It feels so good to be home after ten years.

The (Not So) Winter Wonderland was a huge success for the town and for Dasher Valley High's soccer program. When I asked the players how they were going to spend the money they earned, they answered unanimously that they were getting new tracksuits because Coach Grady and Coach Collins (the girls' head coach) said they believed the team would make it all the way to the state game this season. Lucas's unfiltered joy while watching his players interact with the community and play games with the kids who came through caused my heart to swell three sizes like the Grinch. These past couple of weeks have been like a personal visit from the Ghost of Christmas Past himself, but in a pleasantly blissful way instead of a frightening way. It's like time stood still when I left Mississippi and has now resumed. Little changes prove to me that time has in fact continued. Like the fact that Gracie owns Honey's Café and Bakery now or that Marlee Fletcher came back to this small town after proclaiming she would run far, far away and never look back.

I always thought I would stay, but I was the one who hightailed it out at the offer from Harvard.

But today, being amongst all the community, immersed in the Ghost of Christmas Present—something shifts. The entire paradigm I crafted about Dasher Valley ten years ago when I was panicking about being stuck here forever, married at eighteen...collapsed. A new paradigm is forming. One where I stay and grovel at Lucas's feet for him to have me back, though I'm starting to think it wouldn't take much on my end. One where I visit Gracie at Honey's every day and talk about all the small-town happenings (and convince her to just go on a date with Jared already). A paradigm where I don't have to watch the news every waking moment or act like a snake to get my politician elected. Sure, I love my job. But when you have to spend most of your days consuming news, it gets disheartening and depressing.

I just don't know what else I would do. This is all I've known for the past ten years.

And I will not back out on Mr. Marshall. I intend to break the glass ceiling now. But what comes next?

I can't answer and sleep pulls me under.

G roggy from a restless night full of sugar-induced dreams, I lather on layers of concealer and highlighter. I brush mascara on to give myself the flawless long eyelashes that my brother stole from me and flaunts around.

One particular dream from last night sticks with me like glue on a five-year-old's hand. This is how it went: I never left Mississippi. Lucas was running around the yard—our yard—chasing a toddler with brown curls while shuffling a soccer ball. I stood on the front porch watching with pure love in my eyes while holding our baby girl on my hip.

An immense feeling of pure, unadulterated joy bubbles inside of me, widening my smile and causing me to accidentally glide my nude lipstick across my teeth. It was hard to even care when the dream is tattooed on my brain.

And I want it. I want that reality more than I want to breathe. I often thought about reaching out to Lucas after I first moved to Boston, then to New York—my fingers hovering over the phone for moments on end. Sure, I'd deleted his number, but like the dream, his number is forever stuck with me. The question punches me in the gut often—*what if I would have stayed?* I have no doubt my life would look much like that blissful dream.

But you can't go back to the past. The DeLorean is a mere work of fiction. The paper cuts of the past are stuck there, stinging over and over until the pain turns to numbness, and then settles on disillusionment. It's here to stay. The good, the ugly, and the heart-crippling. The only way to move on is to move forward. To look toward the future.

Shoving the dream to the back burner of my head, I finish getting ready for church.

The smell of bacon, biscuits, and eggs wafts up the stairs, beckoning me down to consume the devilish southern cuisine.

"Mmm." I'm salivating at the mouth like a dog as I make my way down the stairs. "Mama, you've outdone yourself."

"Thanks, darling," a male voice drawls from the kitchen in response. But not just any male voice—the voice of the man starring in my dreams.

"You can't cook, Lucas," I smart off. He mocks offense, setting the spatula in his hand back into the egg pan on the stove.

"Come taste it," he taunts, scooping eggs onto the spatula.

"And ruin a perfectly good morning? No, thank you." He walks toward me holding the spatula and only stops when his face is mere inches from mine. He holds the spatula up to my lips. My body lights up as if on command. Lucas is the stove, and I am the pan. Growing hotter and hotter...

"I said, taste it." His voice is commanding, and I aim to please. *Yes sir.*

Not breaking eye contact, I close my lips around a piece of egg on the spatula.

And moan at the explosion of flavor. Hints of cayenne, onion, garlic, and cheese flood my senses.

"Who can't cook?" Lucas asks, his lips pulling up at one corner. My goodness. I can't with that heavenly face.

"Me. I can't cook," I say between bites. Yes, I'm eating right off the spatula. "Pile a plate for me."

"Yes, ma'am."

I make three cups of coffee while Lucas makes the plates.

"You'll only need two cups. Marian is already at church," he says while setting the plates on the table.

"I'll drink the third cup too, no problem." He nods his head as if agreeing. "Did she drive?"

"No, Brother Johnny picked her up this morning. You just missed her." He shoots me a look, waggling his eyebrows.

"That woman will never retire from her career of flirting."

"Nope, not a chance," he agrees.

We eat in silence, but surprisingly, there is nothing awkward about our silence. It is the kind of silence that signifies true friendship. A comfortable silence. *God, I want to keep this friendship. I don't want to lose Lucas again. Help me not to screw this up.*

TWENTY-TWO

LUCAS

After leaving church, I drive Stella out to Jared's for lunch. He texted me earlier saying he wanted us to come over because he has good news. The long dirt road is muddy from the morning's rain, so my truck is slipping and sliding all over the place. I grip the wheel with white knuckles, curses streaming through my mind. Why hasn't Jared put gravel down on this wretched road yet? Every rut in the road throws Stella against the door, and I've kept up a marathon of apologizing. She keeps telling me not to worry, but I'm pretty sure her face is turning green from the motion of this ride.

Then the truck cuts off right in the middle of a mud hole.

"Sh—oot," I catch myself, remembering I'm in the presence of a lady. Frustration takes over as I hit the steering wheel a few times before launching my body back against the seat. I run my hand through my hair, regretting the day I decided to keep this two-wheel-drive instead of trading it in for a four-wheel drive.

I let out a breath before turning my eyes to Stella, who has been oddly silent. "I am so sorry, Stella."

Yep. I've done went and ruined everything. Stella is fixing to have to get out of the truck in her pretty olive dress and black boots. The color complements her pale skin and freckles way too much to be considered legal. She'll have to step right into the mud. In forty-degree weather. Of course, Mississippi had to pick today to be cold.

"Hold still. After I call Jared, I'll come around and try to get you out without the mud getting on you." The words continue to rush out of my mouth. "I am so, so sorry, Stella."

"Well," she says as though deep in thought. "I don't forgive you."

Oh. I didn't expect that. I mean, I forgave her for leaving me, for crying out loud.

"I don't forgive you." She continues after a pause, "Because you have nothing to be sorry for." She smiles, her nose scrunching up like a cute little elf. She takes her boots off, her Buddy the Elf socks following. Yep, she is an elf. She starts to open the door.

"What are you doing?" I bark. "Hold on! Let me call Jared, then I'll get you."

"I can get myself, thank you very much." And with that, she shoves the door, and it flings open with a series of creaks. Stella gives me one last look before jumping out and sinking into the knee-deep mud. I scramble to take my shoes off and roll up my jeans, then I hop out after her.

The chill of the mud nearly paralyzes my body. She is insane!

As I'm making my way to her side of the truck, a cold, wet thing hits me square in the back. My body goes rigid, and I slowly turn to face my nemesis. Stella is staring wide-eyed as a doe, her mischievous look shifting to panic.

"Lucas, I don't know what I was thinking," she stammers out, trying to walk backward in the thick mud. I bend down, collecting my own glob of mud. "Lucas, please...I didn't mean it!" I raise my arm to fire the deadly shot to her stomach.

But she falls backward instead and becomes fully immersed in the mud. I drop the mud ball and sludge my way over to her, fighting off fits of laughter to be polite.

"Strike two," she says as I reach my hand down to help her up. Her laughter warms the chill encasing my bones.

"When are you going to quit falling for me, Stell Bells?" Her cheeks color despite the cold. She takes my hand, and I wrestle her out of the mud attempting to drag her under. The mud fights back, but with a final jerk, Stella is free and falling onto my chest. A chill runs through her body as it presses into mine. She wraps her arms around me, relaxing into me.

"Let's get you to Jared's," I whisper into her ear. As she steps away from me, the biting air seeps into my skin where her body was.

"Sharing body heat is a survival skill, you know?" Stella looks up at me.

"Get in the truck." My voice grows raspy. "I'll call Jared to come get us." After phoning Jared (and telling him to take his time), I hop into the truck with Stella and turn the heat on.

She takes her cardigan off, and I hand her my extra flannel that is lodged behind my seat. She's still shivering, and quite frankly, I'm on the verge of hypothermia. She looks at me, questioning with her eyes if it's okay to get closer.

"Come here." I gently wrap an arm around her waist and pull her into me. *Thank you, God, for bucket seats.* Stella nestles into my body, and my heart aches at how right our bodies fit together.

"I miss this," she says, closing her eyes and letting her head fall onto my chest. "I miss us."

"Me too," I reply, wondering where reality went. Because it's not here.

"Why didn't you come after me?" she asks, and I hear tears tugging at her voice. What could I say? That I knew Stella like the back of my own hand? That I knew if I would have asked her to stay, she would have? And then she would have resented me our whole lives for it.

"If you love someone, let her go. If she comes back..." That was the advice from my parents. "Momma always said that."

"I loved your momma, but that is a ridiculous saying." She opens her eyes, and I stare down at her upside-down face. "It took some time for me to realize it, but I would have come back. If I only knew..." A single tear pulls at her right eye. I adjust her so that she is sitting up and we are face-to-face.

"I know. Which is why I stayed put. I couldn't take your dreams from you." Stella shakes her head, confirming my suspicions from all those years ago. "But you're here now. After ten years, you're here. I was unbelievably hurt and angry, but I never stopped loving you." Her tear falls. I wipe it away with my hand and leave my hand lingering on her face. Her soft skin warms under my touch, a pink color shining through her done-up face.

She closes her eyes and tilts her chin up. Her lips part slightly, inviting me in. She wants this just as much as I do.

I lean forward, parting my lips and closing my eyes.

They say the kiss is the best part, but no one has ever been enticed to the precipice, hanging on the edge of free fall, by Stella Harper.

Our lips brush lightly, and a million memories associated with these lips swarm my brain. Stella's lips are home. There is not a single doubt. I will follow this woman and her lips wherever she wants to go. My hand slides from her face, twisting into her muddied hair. Her body responds as I deepen the kiss, her hands finding my shoulders and yanking me toward her. Heaven explodes around us.

BEEP! BEEP!

We slowly back away from each other, Stella's eyes reflecting questions as countless as the stars. Neither one of us makes a move to leave the truck.

BEEP! BEEP! BEEP!

"Come on, lovebirds," Jared shouts, hanging out the passenger's side window while Gracie bursts from her seams in the driver's seat.

We fumble our way out of Lucas's truck, sloshing through frigid mud to Jared's truck. All while ignoring the two smiling idiots in the front seat.

Slitting my eyes and putting forth my best scowl, I telepathically growl at Gracie to keep her eyes on the road and not on Stella and me in the backseat of Jared's Ford. Not to mention Jared's continuous peeks through the rearview mirror. I swear he's a sniveling weasel the way he continues to glance into the rearview mirror with a grin the size of Texas on his face.

I sit on the driver's side with my body smashed against the door. Stella sits opposite with her body glued to her door. I imagine we look like elementary kids who refuse to work with someone else of the opposite sex because of cooties. Though we already caught that. A long time ago. Thoughts of her lips on mine run through my mind on repeat, and I inch impossibly closer to the door.

I shouldn't have kissed her. She is leaving to go back to New York. If she asked, I would follow her. I would give up the Athletic Director position. I would give up my family home. I would find a teaching and coaching job in New York.

But she isn't going to ask. For the same reason I didn't ask her to stay. I would give it all up, but in the future, I would grow to resent New York City. I hate cities, and she knows that.

Now what, God? I ask.

Crickets. *Great, thanks.*

TWENTY-THREE

STELLA

The angels in heaven sang a glorious tune. A brief one, but angelic in every sense of the word. Because the moment Lucas's lips met mine, the chorus of "Hallelujah" broke out. Was it stupid? Yes. Was it worth the trouble? Probably not. Am I going to find an opportunity to do that one more time before I leave? You can bet on it.

"Stella and Lucas sitting in a tree, K-I-S-S-I-N-G." Gracie bops around the guest room of Jared's house, taunting me with that song for the gazillionth time. I roll my eyes because asking her politely to stop, then escalating to threats, clearly did nothing. I cinch Jared's baggy gray sweats tighter to fit my waist. I rolled the pants at the ankles five times, yet they still drag on the floor. His matching gray shirt swallows me whole, even with it tucked in at my waist. Don't get me started on my matted hair.

It's official. Lucas is going to regret that kiss after seeing this atrocity of a woman.

"So, was it as good as you remember?" Gracie silences the song in favor of probing questions. Her specialty.

"Better. Much better." In all honesty, it was a thousand times better. "But it was stupid. And the awkwardness sure to follow will ruin this lunch gathering."

"Nothing can ruin this lunch!" Gracie's ecstatic voice prompts questions as she pulls me from the cozy room against my will.

"What are you doing here anyway?" I ask. Did Jared make a move finally? Or did Gracie take the reins like she is known for doing?

"You'll see," she says as we walk into the kitchen.

I catch a glimpse of myself in the reflection of the window. I look like the glob of gray gunk we got on our lunch trays in high school. An atrocious, unappealing sight to behold.

But when we enter the dining room, my mood shifts at the sight of Lucas looking eerily like me (though much more...well, hot. Like really? How does he do that?). He has on a muted gray sweatsuit that is slightly too big for him. The pants are rolled at the waist and ankles. Lucas is several inches taller than me, but we both have nothing on Jared's height. Or Jared's wrestling warmup gear.

We take each other in and let loose the laughter we were straining to hold on to. Maybe it won't be awkward after all.

"Look at us. Just over a week back and we're already twinning." He chuckles and reaches out his hand to me. I take it. It fits perfectly, like his hand is the missing puzzle piece to my body. Something shifted between us in his truck. Whether it was the kiss—something we had done a million and ten times in the past—or the raw truths revealed to each other. Whatever caused the shift, it was for the better.

I feel like I have my best friend back.

"So, what's going on between you two?" I ask between bites of my barbeque chicken. I think there may be saliva running down my chin, but at this point, I couldn't care less. I forgot just how darn good Jared is with a grill.

But I stop mid-bite when Gracie, who had just hopped up to get Jared a refill of lemon water, sets the drink down in front of him, wraps her arms around his shoulders from behind, and plants a kiss on his cheek.

"About dang time," I hear Lucas murmur beside me, a smile in his low voice.

"We could say the same for you two," Jared returns, all while placing a large hand on top of Gracie's arms, which are still wrapped around him.

I turn my eyes to Lucas for a response, but he just smiles and shrugs his shoulders. While I'm ecstatic that nothing feels awkward between us, I know we will have to sit down to have a conversation later about that kiss. But for now...

"All the details," I demand from Gracie. "You too, I want your side." I flick my eyes to Jared. He sits there with a winner's smile while Gracie makes herself at home, apparently permanently attached to his back.

"We know this is sudden," Gracie states, gazing up at Jared with hearts in her eyes. Lucas and I stifle a laugh. No, it's not sudden. We've been impatiently waiting for a while now. Everyone has.

"But Jared came to the coffee shop last night to help me put away things and wash dishes from the (Not So) Winter Wonderland festival, though it was more of him chatting me up than assisting." She glances down at his broken leg. "I don't know if it was the deliriousness of the night or the spiked hot chocolate I made, but we admitted everything to each other."

Jared continues the story. "I told her how I felt. She was silent for a few moments, which had me wanting to run out of the building in humiliation, though that was an impossible option."

"But then I kissed him and realized I never wanted to kiss anyone else. That thought was meant to stay in my head, but I somehow said it out loud." Gracie's smile has never been brighter.

"Then I told her I'll be her last first kiss," Jared turns his face to gaze at Gracie. The amount of love in that single action floors me. It's insane how someone can grow to romantically love another person without dating them, just through years and years of friendship. These two are the hallmark of best friends-to-lovers.

"You guys," I say, becoming Ross from *Friends* when he finds out his best friend is dating his sister. "I'm so happy for you!"

"Again, about time," Lucas pipes in, standing up to bring his empty plate to the sink.

Gracie shrugs and plants a chaste kiss on Jared's lips. "It's the Christmas spirit in the air," she mumbles between pecked kisses with Jared.

"Get a room." Lucas snickers, sitting back down beside me. His hand brushes against mine beneath the table, sending small waves of heat through my body. I don't pull back and our pinkies intertwine.

"Oh, we will soon," Jared comments. "As soon as this leg heals, I'm making Gracie mine forever." Lucas and I exchange wary glances, then my gaze fixes on Gracie, whose mouth is agape. I think Jared put his foot in his mouth, but as soon as the thought enters my mind, Gracie's face lights up brighter than the candle-light on the table. I place my focus back on Lucas, who shifts his body uncomfortably and pulls his hand away to clasp it with his other.

"Well then," I clear my throat, "does anyone have a deck of cards to play Rummy?"

"In the drawer." Jared points to a kitchen drawer. "You may have to dig around." Must be his junk drawer. Gracie bounces to the drawer and finds the cards.

"You're going down," Lucas whispers against my ear, his warm breath tickling my neck.

I turn my face and he's mere inches from me.

"I will retain my title as Rummy Queen," I whisper back, my gaze flicking to his full lips that were on mine not long ago.

"And you were telling us to get a room." Jared cackles. My eyes remain trained on Lucas as we slowly back away from each other. Release floods my body as distance clears my head. *Oh, dear heavens.* How will I leave him again?

*G*o *best friend, that's my best friend,* blares from my phone as I rush to pick it up. I've been swimming in emails for the past two hours. I pick up the phone, noting Hayden's goofy face on the screen. I swipe to answer the FaceTime call.

"Girl, you need sleep," is the first thing she says to me. I can't blame her. It's nearly midnight, but I have to work on the campaign after spending the day with Gracie, Jared, and Lucas. I've been reviewing different campaign ads, talking points, and social media posts. Dark circles haunt my eyes.

"Have you ever been so tired that you couldn't close your eyes? Well, that's me right now." I take another sip of my *fifth* coffee of the day. "Wait, why are you awake?"

"Oh honey, that accent of yours is thicker than it has ever been." She wrinkles her nose. "New York never sleeps, you know that. Anyway, you should give yourself a break. I've got things here. But I get it. This is the biggest opportunity we've had!" A joyful squeal sounds through the phone. I might have joined in on the excited noise a mere two weeks ago. But now? I'm exhausted, confused, and unsure if I want to continue with this career choice.

"Uh-oh." Hayden sees through my fake smile. "What's going on?"

"I'm just tired, that's all."

"You can't lie to me, Stella. What's up?" A genuine smile emerges because I miss this erratic, crazy woman. She truly means the world to me—my first friend in New York.

"Do you remember anything about why I left Mississippi?" I don't remember how much I told her. I kept most of it bottled up and to myself.

"You mentioned you couldn't be tied down. That you had bigger plans. An old fling? But nothing specific, why?"

It's time to come clean to her. With a huff of air, I continue.

"I left because my boyfriend—Lucas Grady—of three years proposed to me a week after our high school graduation."

"Three years is a short time to know each other, huh?" Hayden questions. If she had her way, she'd never settle down. Though I think it's all a façade to keep people at arm's length.

"Not really. Not in southern culture. They marry us off as soon as possible. We went to school together our whole lives. We became friends in the seventh grade, and I kissed him on school grounds in the tenth grade. That one earned me an Out of School Suspension for a day." I sigh at the memory and then remember our most recent kiss. It was good then, but now? Whew. Our kissing matured just as we did. Eighteen-year-old me knew nothing.

"So, this Lucas Grady guy. Is he still where you left him?" Her eyes narrow in suspicion.

"Yeah, he's here. And I kinda kissed him today." Hayden's brown eyes bulge out like she's a squeeze toy. But then a villainous smile overcomes her.

"Tell. Me. Everything," she demands.

And I do, my body heating up with every detail.

TWENTY-FOUR

STELLA

I rub the knot that formed in my neck from slouching over my computer all morning. Campaign managers do not get Christmas Eve off, unfortunately. I pick up the coffee cup in front of me and bring it to my lips. Except nothing comes out. *Sigh.*

"Need a refill?" Gracie's sing-song voice breaks through my dismay. She holds a fresh pot in her hands.

"My hero." I grin up at her, handing her my coffee cup with both hands like it's my most prized possession. She fills it up, then sets the pot on my table before sliding into the booth beside me. I grab a gingerbread cookie from the plate in front of me and take a delicious, spicy bite. At that time, Mama walks into the cafe with Brother Johnny Howell at her side. I catch her attention and wave them over.

"Hey Ms. Marian, Brother Johnny." Gracie waves, sliding out of the booth. "Can I get you something?"

"I see you have a pot of coffee here, so two cups would be great," Mama replies, embracing Gracie in a quick hug.

"On the way." She bounces toward the counter.

"What are you crazy kids up to this Christmas Eve morning?" I take a sip of my coffee and purse my lips at the bitter taste. Mama laughs and scoots the sugar and creamer my way.

"Always looking out for me, Mama," I hum, shaking sugar into the bitter, black liquid. Gracie returns, her blonde curls bouncing, with two coffee cups. She slides back into the booth beside me.

"You'll always be my baby girl." Mama's eyes sparkle. "We were just stopping in for a cup of coffee before picking up a few toys to bring to Hannah's Hope. They will be passing out the toys to parents tonight who need extra assistance." She pours Brother Johnny a cup of coffee before pouring herself the rest of the pot.

"That's sweet," I say. "Mrs. Phyllis was donating the money made from her Pineapple Jambalaya to Hannah's Hope."

"It's a much-needed place," Gracie chimes in while picking up a gingerbread cookie from the plate in front of us.

"Indeed. Our church partners with them," Brother Johnny mentions.

"Let me know how I can be of assistance," I say. "I have plenty of connections."

"Will do, Miss Stella." He tips his head toward me.

"Please, Brother Johnny." I laugh, "Don't call me *miss*. You've known me since I was in diapers!"

He takes a sip of his coffee, then eyes Mama. A silent conversation passes between them, while memories of Dad flood over me. Mama and Dad used to have those silent conversations too.

"So, Mama." I clear my throat, trying to check Mama's ring finger. Her hands are under the table, so no such luck. "Any other Christmas Eve plans?"

"Just the Christmas Eve service tonight." Mama smiles up at Brother Johnny.

"Are you coming, Stella?" he asks.

"Of course! I'll be there. Wouldn't miss it!"

I'm transported to all the Christmas Eve church services in the past as I set foot into the small, country church. I went to church as much as I could in New York, but my job kept me busy most Sundays.

The green Douglas Firs stand erect on both sides of the altar, boasting their needles, decor, and lights. Poinsettias, my favorite type of Christmas flower, line the pews. Mama is already sitting in the front row, and I make my way to her thinking I'll have to be a front row Baptist for the night since she is dating the pastor.

I slide in beside her, take her hand, and give it a squeeze. She smiles gently at me and then looks beyond me. Lucas walks up and asks if he can sit with us. Of course, Mama says yes, and I nod my head enthusiastically.

Man, he looks so good dressed up. If one can call a flannel dressed up, that is. But he wears slacks with his flannel, the shirt is tucked in, and he's wearing black dress shoes.

Be still my heart.

"How's it feel being back here for Christmas?" he whispers against my ear. His voice is like a gentle caress, sending feelings through me that I shouldn't be having while sitting in the house of the Lord.

"It feels..." I breathe in. Out. "Good. So very good." *Home. I'm home.*

Brother Johnny welcomes everyone from the pulpit, and the service begins with "O Holy Night"—one of my favorite Christmas hymns.

My heart is full. It's right where it longs to be and that thought terrifies me.

TWENTY-FIVE

LUCAS

Stella and I stand in the middle of the Dasher Valley High soccer field, no lights but the stars above us. It's a rather warm night for December, but a slight wind offers a bit of a chill. A perfect night for stargazing, picnicking...and kissing, if I have it my way.

"We need to talk." Stella breathes as she spreads a quilt on top of the grass. My heart picks up at the four words no man wants to hear.

I try to stall Stella's impending speech, knowing all too well she is about to tell me that we have to stop acting like a couple because she's going to go back to New York City.

I don't want to hear it.

After placing the red wine, cheese, and meats on the blanket, I gesture for her to sit. She eases down to rest on her knees, her evergreen dress spreading around her. I sit down behind her, prepared to stall the mess out of this conversation.

My hands trail from her elbows up her sleeved arms, secretly loving the feel of the silky fabric, until I pause at her shoulders. I rub my thumbs into her shoulders, finding quite a few knots. She moans, letting her head fall forward so I can get the back of her neck. A chill runs through my body that has nothing to do with the slight wind. I know she's been busy with the campaign, working into the wee hours of the morning. A part of me feels guilty because I've kept her from her work the past few days. But then again, she has forever to work on those campaigns.

I, however, only have this small window of time that God has blessed me with. Or tortured me with. I can't quite decide.

"Lucas," she sighs my name, then reaches up with both hands to her shoulders and takes my hands into her own. "It's been so very nice seeing you again." She rubs circles on my hands. The warmth of her skin on my rough hands sends flames licking through my body. "Your forgiveness took so many chips off my shoulders. I spent years wondering what would happen if I saw you again."

"If?" I question.

"Yes, if," she breathes. "I had no intention of seeing you again."

"At least you're honest," I huff, turning my face away.

"I had no intentions because I couldn't face the fact that you would hate me." Disbelief stuns me into silence for a moment. I look back into her eyes.

"How could I ever hate you, Stella Harper?" I respond, clutching her hands in mine. "I was angry, of course. But hate?" I scoff. "I couldn't hate you, Stella. Never. You have always been home to me."

"If I hadn't left as abruptly as I did, would you have considered coming to New York with me?" Her eyes are desperate, searching for validation. What will she think of my answer?

"I think..." I begin. "I think, given some time to reflect and plan, that I would have gone with you."

"I don't know if that makes me happy or sad," she comments, eyes cast down. I pull my hands away from hers and tuck stray hairs behind her ears. My hands rest on her cheeks, gently guiding her face upward toward mine.

"The past is just that, Stella. We can learn to keep it there." She pulls back slightly, eyes flitting back and forth, searching mine.

"One thing hasn't changed," she says softly. "I love you." My heart flips. "I never stopped."

"Can I kiss you?" I ask, though my hands are already tugging her face toward mine. Her words twirl around my mind. When we are mere inches apart, her breath hitches.

"W-wait," she stutters out. I stop, dropping my hands. "You need to know the kiss we shared yesterday wasn't from a place of nostalgia or loneliness. It was from the deepest parts of my soul. The way I feel about you."

"I know," I whisper. "I felt it." Hesitancy flashes in her eyes, and I realize what I've done wrong in this situation.

"I love you, too, Stella. You brilliant, beautiful, woman."

Her lips crash into mine, melting and molding to my form. I let her lead, soaking in our confessions, letting them seep into my DNA. Her hands wrap around my neck and pull me closer. My hands find her hips, clutching the silky fabric. I trace my hands up her back as her lips work against mine, until I tangle my hands into her hair.

After a moment, she pulls back, breathless, her lips still very near to mine. Any chill in the air has dissipated. I drop my hands from her hair to her shoulders, sliding my hands down until I find her trembling hands.

"What do we do about this?" I ask. My heart aches at the thought of her leaving me again. I don't know if I could get on with my life this time around.

"I–I don't know." Soft tears collect in her eyes. "But we don't have to figure it out tonight."

With that, I claim her lips for my own again.

TWENTY-SIX

STELLA

"But we don't have to figure it out tonight," I stutter out, and Lucas silences any other words. His familiar lips are on mine, exploring hesitantly. I bring my hands to the collar of his Christmas red flannel and wrap them into fists, dragging his upper body closer to me. He takes the signal and deepens the kiss. It's a kiss of lost time, pain, and immense joy. A kiss that signifies he knows me. He knows my lips and where to place his hands—one on the small of my back and the other wrapped in my hair. He knows my deepest fears, my best-kept secrets, and the nasty side to my personality. Lucas knows me. And I know him. This kiss is the ghost of a thousand lost kisses we missed these past ten years.

Eventually pulling back for air, I can't help but imagine what would happen if I stayed here. Or if he came to New York with me. I imagine the kids of my dreams. The big backyard. The life we could create together.

I collapse to the ground, falling onto my backside, and tuck my knees to my chest.

"What do we do about this?" I repeat his earlier question. Guilt eats at me, knowing I have to leave, yet I'm kissing him like I want nothing more in the world than to stay. Which, at this moment, is particularly true. His chest heaves up and down, golden brown eyes still wild with need, as he kneels in front of me.

"You could work from here," he suggests, still collecting his breath. "I mean, you've been doing it since you've been home." I think about it for a moment, but there is still a part of me that wants to be in the city for this work. It's so much easier to be able to sit down with my team in person. I haven't enjoyed working virtually like this.

"I prefer being in person with my team," I say. "Would it be so wrong for you to consider moving to New York?" His silence answers my question.

"Stella, I—" he begins, and I turn my face away. I don't want him to see the tears about to fall. "I have an established life here. I think I have a great shot at the Athletic Director's position, due in part to your help with the festival."

"And I have an established life in New York," I sigh, defeated. Why in the world would God bring us together like this just to rip our souls apart again? *Why,* I question Him. *I know Your plans are good. Your ways are higher. But why?*

"So this is really it, huh?" he asks, twisting off his knees and rolling over to lie on his back, hands tucked beneath his head. I lie on my side, my elbow propping me up so that I can see him.

"Long distance?" I chuckle even as I suggest it.

"I think it's now or never with us, Stell Bells."

"Let's think about it later." I place my free hand on his chest, and he shudders under my touch. "Tonight is ours."

"We would be celebrating nine years married tonight," he says. My heart clenches, and I sit up.

"I wonder what those years would have looked like?" I muse. He sits up and pulls his phone out of his back pocket. "You should really upgrade your phone."

He shakes his head with a slight laugh and continues doing whatever it is he's doing. Before I know it, the opening chords of Nat King Cole's rendition of the "The Christmas Song" plays and tears well in my eyes. He stands up, reaches down to take my hand, and helps me up.

Slowly, he wraps one arm around my waist and takes my hand with the other. He sways with me as the music plays, holding me close and with gentle care as if I'm a China doll that will break with the slightest pressure.

"This would have been our first dance," he whispers against my ear. My body clings close to his. I close my eyes, fully immersing myself in the moment. We had discussed long before we were engaged that we wanted a Christmas Eve wedding and this song to be our first dance.

We sway, bodies attached like glue, as the rest of the song plays.

When it ends, he hits replay. This time, I stare into his eyes which remind me of sunshine, darkened by the night. Our foreheads touch, lips lingering inches apart. We sway together, our movements as one.

What was meant to be our first dance as a married couple is becoming our last before parting ways again.

"Want to eat?" I ask after finishing the song again. I need a moment to breathe. Having him so close, knowing he isn't mine to have, is utterly crushing.

"Yes, I'll pour the wine, you get the meat and cheese," he says, already busying himself.

We sit and snack under the stars, saying nothing while listening to Sinatra's Christmas songs, each finishing off two glasses of wine before we speak again.

"I want to dance with you again," I finally say, climbing to my feet. I slip my black booties off and make my way to the field to feel the dead grass beneath my feet. If tonight is all I have, then I want it. I want it for the most selfish of reasons. Lucas—my high school sweetheart, my ex-fiancé, the most respectable man I know—is here in front of me after ten years. I love him. He loves me. And we have Christmas Eve.

This is decidedly a very merry Christmas.

Cinnamon rolls dance in my dreams. So delicious, so hot and flaky, so sweet...such a strong smell.

My eyes flicker open, and I realize I'm staring at the roof over my childhood bed. I don't remember coming back here. I remember dancing with Lucas on the soccer field until we were in a fit of giggles and could dance no longer. I remember sitting on the quilt

Grandma gave me before she passed away. I remember sipping on red wine and eating cheese. I remember one glass...two glasses...three.

Oh no. There must have been more than three.

I remember kissing and dancing. Lots and lots of kissing. Kissing while swaying under the stars. Kissing on our knees in the grass. Kissing in his truck. Kissing on my bed...

Violently throwing myself out of bed, I scan my room like I'm on the lookout for my campaign's rival candidate. Everything looks normal. I'm in my Grinch onesie that I wear every Christmas. There is no sign of Lucas. No sign of...anything else out of the ordinary.

But the smell of cinnamon rolls is vivid and beckons me.

I let my nose lead me out of my room and down the stairs, my stomach rumbling the entire way.

"Someone's hungry," a male voice calls out from the vicinity of the kitchen. I don't need to look in a mirror to know my frizzy hair is sticking out like a lion's mane or that my makeup from the Christmas Eve service last night is still on my face and smeared. I don't need a mirror to know my face is turning the color of cranberries at the moment.

Lucas Grady.

Is cooking cinnamon rolls.

In my mama's house.

On Christmas morning.

I run back up the stairs because he cannot see me like this. Plus, I have about five seconds to jar my memory of last night before I absolutely lose my freaking mind!

"God, I'm sorry," I cry, guilt settling in. "He isn't mine, and boy, I acted like he was mine." *Please, please, please, let it have been just kissing. I'm sorry, God, I'm sorry.*

My phone buzzes somewhere in my room. I hunt it down, finding it underneath my bed.

Hayden is FaceTiming me, while the man I spent all night kissing (presumably) is downstairs cooking breakfast, while I look like a hungover sorority girl (which I'm definitely acting like).

Merry freaking Christmas.

Sincerely, your favorite no good, confused, guilty Grinch.

"Merry Christmas!" Hayden shouts as her face pops onto the screen. Her words attack my head like a sledgehammer. I put my finger to my lips.

"You look like death," she says, her voice several octaves lower.

"It was an...eventful night."

"Oooh, do tell." She wiggles her eyebrows. "Does this night have anything to do with Lucas Grady?" I feel heat flooding my cheeks, giving me away. She nods, making a humming sound.

"I'm still trying to figure out what happened." I laugh in disbelief. We had already admitted our feelings to each other, but last night...it felt like high school nights all over again. I was a child, giddy and helpless against the man's wiles. Feminine wiles? Ha. You've never met Lucas Grady.

"You look really happy, Stells." Hayden's voice grows soft, her eyes sparkling.

"I am," I sigh. "But I've got to get over it. I leave in two days."

"I'll have ice cream ready for you when you return," she says. "Chocolate chip cookie dough." I throw my head back in laughter. Leave it to Hayden to brighten my sour mood.

"This is why I love you."

"I love you too, Stells."

"Merry Christmas, Hayden," I say, clicking off the phone, already resorting back to being a Sour Patch Kid. Why, oh why? I've gone and done the one thing I wasn't supposed to do—fall back in love with Lucas Grady. I drop my phone to the floor and throw myself onto my hordes of pillows, letting out the loudest grunt I can muster.

And of course, that is when Lucas chooses to walk into my room.

TWENTY-SEVEN

LUCAS

"Dang, Stell Bells. You sound like you're maxing out on squats." Laughter forces its way out of her, and now my brain has images of Stella squatting in her Nike shorts. I always spotted her in high school. I'd be her spotter again. Safety first, right?

"My body feels like I have." She groans again, shoving a pillow over her face. Something is bothering her. "Tell me what's going on," I press. She doesn't move but mumbles something that sounds like "phone". I pick up her phone from the floor by her bed. I remove the pillow from her face and get the urge to lean over and kiss her, even though we kissed the night away last night. It'll never be enough.

"Stella, what's up?" I press again.

"You do know I leave in two days, right?" Yes, I do. Though, a smidge of hope planted itself in my chest last night, begging her to stay.

I nod my head.

"Just checking," she says. "What...what happened last night? Why are you here?"

"We just kissed, Stella," I reassure her. "Remember, we said we wouldn't do more than that until our wedding night." The memory of *that* conversation so many years ago rushes in. "A lot of kissing, but that's it."

She breathes a sigh of relief, and I can't help but wonder something. "Have you...you know..." She stares at me like I have an extra head or something. Maybe I shouldn't have asked that question.

"Oh, gosh no, Lucas! I meant what I said all those years ago. *Sex* is sacred," she finally says the word I wouldn't, a grin tugging at her lips. "And you?"

"I haven't." I try to laugh, but the sound comes out more like a choked cow. Whatever that sounds like. It's been easy to save myself. No woman has ever tempted me like Stella does.

Shaking off that awkward conversation, I fill her in on why I'm here already. "I came over early to get breakfast started because I know Marian wasn't feeling too well last night at church."

"You are such a good, wonderful man, Luca," she says. Those words should elate me, but all they do is remind me that she is once again choosing not to be mine.

"What if you didn't go?" The words spew out of my mouth. I thought I got her all out of my system last night, but my feelings for her are much stronger now. I can't handle watching her walk out of my life again. I've only just healed from the first time.

"Lucas, please. Don't say that. Do not plant that seed." A single tear gathers at the edge of her misty gray eyes. "You know I can't."

"I do, which is why I would never ask that of you." My heart feels like it's shattering into glass splinters. Broken Heart Syndrome is a real thing, something I learned in my years of teaching Biology, and dang it, it sucks. I knew better than to say that. And I would never ask her to. *If you love someone, let them go...*

More tears leak from her beautiful eyes, and I pull her into my arms. She holds on for a moment before letting go and whispering "Merry Christmas" into my ear, and then she slides out of my arms.

I head downstairs to let her get dressed.

It's Christmas morning, and I feel like crap. Like every other Christmas morning for the past ten years. Once again, I've done something to cause Stella pain. The first thing? Proposing to her while we were only eighteen. I made her choose between me and her career. Now? It's like I am doing the same thing again. Ten years later, a second chance, and I still can't get it right? *Why?* I question God. I know better than to do that, but sometimes I just have to scream it out...even if it is only mentally.

Plopping down on the couch after making coffee to go with the cinnamon rolls for the Harper women, I turn on the TV.

Marian hobbles into the room. She's been having a bad time this week, so I came over to help out this morning. I know Stella has been looking forward to her first Christmas in a long time with her mother. Stone has been visiting with friends and a new girl he has been seeing down here. I told him to go out and have fun when he asked me if I needed his help.

"What happened with you and Stella last night?" Marian questions, her eyes squinting at me. "You brought her home quite late."

"I'm sorry, Marian," I mutter, feeling ashamed under her gaze. *Oh, I kissed your daughter until we both couldn't think straight or remember our own names last night. But don't worry, nothing else happened!*

"Nothing to be sorry for," Marian says cracking a smile, surprising me. "I've been praying for that girl to come to her senses and make her way back home for years. I'm proud of her, don't get me wrong. But I knew in my soul she wasn't completely happy. Mark my words. Love is worth so much more than career and fame." I sit there, soaking in her words. Stella comes down the stairs, looking made up again like she is scared to show her true self.

I miss the Grinch onesie.

Stone follows behind her in sweatpants, a Juniper Grove University football t-shirt, and disheveled hair.

"Merry Christmas," I'm greeting both, but I'm mainly talking to Stella. I was so distracted that I forgot to say those two simple words earlier. But my words don't sound merry or cheerful or holly or jolly. They sound strained.

Stella offers a hesitant smile while Stone pushes her to get down the stairs faster because there are "cinnamon rolls with my name on them," as he said. We all laugh at his shenanigans, but Stella, Marian, and I exchange conflicted looks.

What is the fallout from my late-night, Christmas Eve confession?

I may lose Stella Harper. Again. Forever.

TWENTY-EIGHT

STELLA

This is the first Christmas that I have celebrated at home where I'm not wearing some sort of Christmas pajamas or onesies. After Winegate last night, I have to protect myself. The only way I know to do that is to paint my face with my warrior makeup, put on a cute outfit, and do my hair up in curls—teasing it to the high heavens because I am a southern-bred woman. If I look good, then I will feel good. At least that is the theory. It's not working out that way.

The cinnamon rolls are delicious, though. And that counts for something.

We all sit around the table meant for five, but it's missing one of our own—Dad. Though we were a family of four, Dad insisted we always have a place for a guest at our table. That is what Mama told Stone and me every time we asked for a smaller table after Dad passed away. Except she added that we had a place for two guests now, and Dad would be so proud of us for working through the pain with joy. So, we did, and it was hard. We had very bad days, but we also had days where people would come over, sit in Dad's spot, and all was right in the world.

It never gets easier though. Especially at holidays like Christmas. Stone keeps us entertained through breakfast—helping me more than he could ever realize.

"So, who's ready for presents?" Stone's blue eyes light up. He was the baby of the family and it still shows on days like today.

"Me first," I say, wandering over to the tree and pulling out Mama's gift.

I hand her the card wrapped in Christmas paper and watch intently as her fragile hands shake while they open it.

"You didn't have to get me anything, Stella. You are my favorite gift," Mama protests, but she continues to open it. After a moment, she has the paper off and flicks the card open. Two tickets to New York float down to the ground. I pick them up for her and wait for her to finish reading the card. I don't quite remember what I wrote, as I did this when I purchased my own ticket home, but I do remember it has something to do with how I want her to experience my life in New York...if just once in her life.

She looks up from the card with tears pricking at the corners of her eyes. Without a word, she hugs me. I wrap her in my arms and tears start forming in my own eyes. What did I write on that card?

When she pulls free, I hand her the two tickets.

"I know you don't want to move to New York, but I would love for you to visit me through the new year."

"But why two tickets?" she asks, confused.

"I don't know..." I let my eyes wander lazily. "Just thought you would want a travel companion on the way home. You can have your pick of people—Stone, Lucas, or *Brother. Johnny.*" I add the last one looking directly at her, hoping to elicit a blush. Nothing. The woman is unabashed and unashamed.

"Wonderful." She grins. "I'll call him up now and see if he's free. The twenty-seventh, huh? Two days away. I've got a lot to do!" I'm stunned at her joy over this, and it thrills me that she is finally saying yes to visiting me in NYC. Maybe I just needed to purchase the tickets myself this entire time. Or the promise of Brother Johnny tagging along is enough for her. I chuckle under my breath at Mama acting like a giddy teenager who gets to run off on a vacation with her boyfriend. She hobbles out of the room to grab her phone from the kitchen charger.

"No tickets for me?" Stone asks, bringing his hand to his heart like he is wounded.

"Please. You've been several times. It's Mama's turn."

"You're right. I've got plans for New Year's Day anyway." He winks, and I roll my eyes at his playboy lifestyle.

"But I did get you something." I hand him a football wrapped in Christmas paper.

"A football?"

"Open it." I watch his eyes bulge out at the signed football from his favorite player—Drew Brees.

"I love your connections." He flips the ball around in his hands before embracing me in a bear hug that lifts my feet off the ground for the second time since he's been home. My ankle has been healing nicely, so I only wince a little at the prick of pain.

"I'm a broke college kid," Stone says. "So I got you this JGU sweatshirt from the bookstore." I laugh, assuring him I love it. And I do, because sweatshirts are absolute life.

He bounces out of the room to give Mama her gift after giving Lucas a JGU flannel. Stone may be a player with the ladies, but he has a heart of gold. He just has to find the right girl that he can commit to.

Lucas and I stand by the tree, looking everywhere but at each other.

The once comfortable silence has turned immensely awkward.

"I got you a gift," we both blurt at the same time, which elicits laughter from the both of us.

"Me first," I say. I bend down under the tree to find the stack of journal entries that I ripped out of my journal a couple of nights ago. I shoved them in a box and tied them with a pretty bow. "You can't open it here. Wait until I go back to New York, please." His eyes are loaded with questions, but he nods and salutes.

"Scout's honor." I laugh at his antics. "Now, my turn." We both grow serious because a seismic shift took place last night, and I'm not prepared to acknowledge it or what this gift could be.

He reaches into his back pocket and pulls out a small box. My insides grow hard, terrified of what's in that box. I look everywhere but his eyes, willing myself to breathe in through my nose and out through my mouth. It can't possibly be what my brain is telling me it is. There is no way.

"I know this is a bit far-fetched." Lucas fiddles with the box, tossing it back and forth between seemingly nervous hands. "But I couldn't think of another woman to give this to, so I—"

"Lucas. Stop. I—I can't." I place a shaking hand on his chest, willing his eyes to meet mine. A flash of confusion washes through his radiant brown eyes. "I can't go there again..." I try to show both my desire for him and the pain and anxiety I'm working through in my eyes.

Except he looks like he's working overtime to suppress a laugh.

"Open it, Stella." I melt, lost in his eyes and the sugary sweetness of his southern voice.

I open the box with trembling hands. Tears are already forming in the corners of my eye. I tried to warn him... I can't stay.

"Luca!" All sense of worry, dread, and anxiety float away at the sight of the gingerbread man stud earrings. They are the cutest Christmas earrings I have ever seen.

"You thought I was proposing." His laugh bursts through his held-together exterior. My whole body heats up with embarrassment, but then I join in his laughter. No matter how badly I just embarrassed myself, I am one hundred percent relieved he did not do what I thought he was going to do. After last night...

"Okay, okay. I admit it. But seriously, these are adorable!" I take out the golden hoops I have in and put on the studs. "I'll cherish them forever." I give Lucas a hug, aching at how much he feels like home.

We spend the rest of the day laughing, enjoying great food that we all helped cook (and I didn't burn), and cherishing the time left together. No matter what happens, this is my favorite Christmas *ever*.

TWENTY-NINE

STELLA

S ad Taylor Swift music blares through my Air Pods as I sit in the truck with Stone. He volunteered to drive me back to the airport. I refused to ask Lucas. After saying goodbye earlier, I couldn't stand the thought of him driving me the two and half hours back to the airport. If I had seen his face again, I would have broken down and never left.

And I couldn't do that. I have to go back. I have the campaign to win for Mr. Marshall. He is counting on me. My team is counting on me. The game is politics, and I know how to play.

I watch the trees on the side of the highway pass by in a blurry green wall. "All Too Well" (the ten-minute version) plays on repeat. This is the fourth time I've played it.

A tap on my shoulders pulls me away from my dreary truck window crying.

"Why are you leaving, Stella?" Stone bluntly asks. He has never been one to shy away from speaking whatever crosses his mind.

"Because I have a presidential campaign to manage and a life in New York to get back to."

"I get the campaign, but why do you care so much about leaving Mississippi and your family?" Ouch, kid.

"I'll come back more. Especially after this campaign is over," I say matter-of-factly.

"But what happens after?"

"That's what I have to figure out." I inhale a steadying breath, turning to looking out of the window again.

"For the record, I think you're happier at home." A sad laugh escapes my tightly pressed lips. He sees right through me.

"You've only seen me in New York like three times," I scoff, deterring the too truthful insight coming out of his mouth.

"Yeah, and that was enough. You're happier here, *Stell Bells*."

"Why is that, *brother*?"

"Lucas Grady." I bite my bottom lip. Yes. He makes me happy, giddy like a schoolgirl, but so does my career. *Keep telling yourself that,* my soul whispers. I ignore it.

When we arrive at the airport, Stone helps me gather my bags, then he hugs me goodbye. Never have I felt so hesitant to get on a plane. My mind flashes to ten years ago, standing in this very spot in front of the terminal to Boston. I was swarming with excitement to leave. I couldn't leave fast enough. Looking back, I know it was because if I didn't go then, I never would. Now, standing here ready to fly to New York City, the very city I've lived in since I finished college, I'm not sure I want to go back.

"Welcome home!" Hayden's squeal penetrates my sullen mood. No, New York doesn't feel like home anymore, but Hayden does. Right now, I am extra thankful for this spirited, fun human being. She wraps me in a hug that feels like a cold morning by a fireplace in cozy socks.

"Hey," I manage to croak out while holding back tears that threaten my eyes again.

"Wow, even your 'hey' sounds southern thick," she comments. I shrug, knowing I will have to fight off the thickness of the accent again. "You're down. What's wrong?"

The tears come gushing out as I stand in the middle of the JFK airport.

I melt into her arms, letting her hold me up.

"You love him, don't you?" Hayden strokes my wild hair. I never bothered to fix it before leaving.

"I do," I whisper against her chin.

"Then why are you here?"

"Commitment. My life here. You."

"While I am much obliged, I can still be friends with you in Mississippi, you know. Though don't tell anyone," she jests. "I understand you don't want to back out on Darcy. I mean, who would? Just look at him!" I pull away from her, side-eying her at her comment.

"I thought he was grumpy and rough," I say.

"He is. But you can't deny his looks." We both laugh together. Me through sniffles, of course.

"I'll be okay. I forgot him one time. I can do it again."

"But did you really forget him the first time?" she asks, seeing right through me as usual.

"No, I didn't." I shake my head. "But I did get myself to a place where I was okay. And I can do that again."

"I know you can, Stells. And you've always got me." I smile at the wonderful woman and wipe the tears away.

We go get my luggage from the baggage claim, and a depressing storm cloud settles over my soul.

THIRTY

LUCAS

The ball bounces off the wall and back into my hand for the millionth time. I don't know how long I've been lying in bed, throwing the tennis ball at the wall...but my arm is numb, so pretty long. With every bounce, I mentally kick myself for not buying a ticket and traveling to New York with her. No matter what she protested.

But I know she was right. I would love the beginning—just being with Stella. Eventually, I would grow to despise her for making me stay there and leave the comfort of what I know. Cheers to kicking off the New Year.

Alone.

Again.

There was something, though. She wanted to stay here. I saw it in her eyes. She felt at home. I felt complete. I was fully and permanently happy. The kind of happy you can only be when you are with the one your soul smiles for.

That's it.

Grabbing the wrapped box she gave me for Christmas, I tear it open. Why did I wait so long to open it? Because I've been trying to forget her, once again. But I don't want to forget her anymore.

A wooden box lies beneath the Christmas tree wrapping paper. I lift the lid from the box and immediately hold my breath. Letters...so many letters. I sort through them, looking at the dates. Letters that go back to 2012 through 2018. Some are short, some are long. All of them are written by Stella and addressed to me—Luca. Tears push to the front of my eyes as I begin to read. Phrases like *I miss you* and *I still love you* and *why can't I just forget you* repeat in many of the letters. Raw and honest journals kept from Stella to me while she was in New York over the past six years. Was 2018 when she finally got over me?

A note taped to the bottom of the box catches my eye.

To: Luca

From: Stell Bells

Nearly tearing it out of the box, I open it.

I prayed I would never see you again. I knew if I did that I would be a goner. Well, I was right about one thing in life. What was I wrong about? Ha, where to begin? I was wrong that life in New York City would satisfy my deepest desire of changing the world. I was wrong that I couldn't have an impact in little ole Dasher Valley, Mississippi. Watching you with your soccer boys...you have such a big heart and they look up to you in so many ways. You are making a greater impact than I ever could. I was wrong to think that I would rot away if I didn't escape at eighteen. I was wrong to leave you without so much as a reason and goodbye. I was wrong that you couldn't give me the life I wanted. Luca, I am an idiot for running away from you and my home all of those years ago. Yes, it brought me to where I am today, and it was all a part of God's plan, but I fear it's too late for us. Is it? Is it too late for us? Will you move to New York? Will I move home—back to Mississippi? I don't know. I have so many questions and conflictions. One thing I do know? I love you. I never stopped. Are these letters proof enough?

Can second chances really happen? Or is that the work of romance writers? Can we do this?

I have to stay and see out my commitments through the New Year. I have Darcy Marshall's campaign. But what comes after? Help me decide. I pray I hear from you, Luca. Do we get a second chance?

I pull out my phone and call Jared. It's New Year's Eve *eve*, so he's probably with Gracie. I need their help. Primarily Gracie's help because she is always on my side.

"**W**hat's up, bro?" Jared asks on the other end of the line.

"I need you to talk me out of something. Is Gracie there?" The words rush out of my mouth.

"Uh-huh." I can virtually see his eyebrows knotting together at my insane request and tone of voice, even though we aren't using FaceTime.

"Here!" Gracie shouts.

"I'm on the edge of buying a ticket to New York City."

"Then go!" I hear Gracie shout in the background. I knew she'd be on speaker. And I knew she would tell me to go. Jared shushes her in the background.

"Look, man. As much as I want to let Gracie take over this conversation, you are still my best guy. And I have to look after you. She crushed you, bro. Are you sure you are ready for that to happen again?"

I'm silent because my answer is both yes and no. I'm not as broken as I was when she left ten years ago, but that doesn't mean that I'm not hurting this time. I am. But I'm also tired.

"I'm tired of missing her. I'm tired of dating just to compare every woman to her. It's not fair to them or me. I'm tired of thinking she'll come back. I'm tired of asking myself the big stupid 'what if' question." Weight lifts off my shoulder with the confession. I truly didn't realize just how tired I was. "And I think she feels the same way."

"Then go," Jared repeats his girlfriend's words. "Better yet. I'll buy the ticket."

"No man, you don't have to do that. I got it."

"Consider it a Christmas gift, Lucas," Gracie shouts again.

"What she said." Jared laughs.

"Okay, okay," I sigh, feeling an overwhelming sense of content-ment. "Let's do this."

I find myself standing in the Jackson airport once again in under a month's time. Except now, I'm begging and pleading with God to get me to New York before midnight, instead of dreading picking up the woman who once held my heart. Gracie casually slipped Stella's address to me, since I never bothered to ask before she left. I didn't want to get Marian's hopes up, so she doesn't know anything is going on. She is enjoying herself already in New York, I'm sure.

After checking my bags, I wait in the terminal. The lady next to me glares and I realize I'm shaking all the seats in my row with my insistent leg bouncing. I stop, but then my hands continually fidget with my jacket. My hair. The seat. My jeans.

I've been working on my speech. The entire way here (thanks to Jared and Gracie driving me), I kept testing out what to say with Gracie, to which she kept replying, "Just say what's on your heart, Lucas. Stella wants nothing more than that."

There is so much on my heart though. My brain is so full of words I want to say to her that I may word vomit them out at first glance. No. I need to be smoother than that. More New York-ish. Suave. I think that's what they call smooth men?

They finally call for boarding and I make my way to the plane. Middle seat. Fun.

I toss my headphones on, letting George Strait take over. He will have words for me to say.

THIRTY-ONE

LUCAS

I already despise New York City and its crowd. Maybe it's because it's New Year's Eve? I doubt it. But what do I know?

The bustling city sprawls on and on before my eyes. The streets have been shut down for all the events, so I find myself wading through crowds to get to Stella's apartment complex. Why does she have to live in the middle of the city? My heart constricts while walking through the crowds, my breathing growing hard and heavy. Every way I turn, there are people and stages. And plenty of the people are completely drunk.

Not to mention that no one waits for the walk signal. Come on, guys. I'm not looking to be roadkill.

I continue following the GPS on my phone that's taking me to her apartment via walking directions with only my small duffle bag in tow. Two hours after I stepped foot out of the cab from the airport (which I despised as well), I find myself at the entrance of Stella's complex. The building is old but has been renovated with modern decor. As with other buildings in this city, it expands upward versus outward—as if it is taunting me for even gracing its doorstep. My heart speeds up again, and I suddenly have every desire to turn around, walk two hours through the crowds again, and find myself a cab. I think I'd rather walk around New York City ten times over than do what I'm about to do.

But I came here with one sole purpose—to win Stella Harper back (and pray she wants to come back to a slower life with me). It's selfish, I know. But I have to ask. I couldn't do it over the phone or text. I couldn't wait, either, for her to come around again. I had to come here, to her life. I had to show her I'm serious. I'm serious about her.

The sun has set, the already bone-chilling cold has become even colder, and every second is inching closer to midnight.

I walk into the building and take the elevator up to the eleventh floor (the top floor)—a rather short building for New York City. I step off, turn around to face the elevator, and watch the doors close. After a deep breath, I turn away and walk toward 11G.

This is it. The moment that will free me. She'll either agree and come back to Mississippi with me, or she will shut me out. If she chooses to shut me out, I'll accept it. I will go back home, take some time to heal, and move on. For good. Of course, I really don't want to go through that healing, so here's to praying she likes the first option.

I ring the doorbell that has a mini wreath circling it. I wait, sweating bullets down my face despite the chill in the air. No answer. I ring the doorbell again. After waiting a minute, I ring it one last time.

No answer.

Maybe this is God's way of telling me that I just need to go home. She either isn't home or she's ignoring me. Though, Stella shouldn't know I'm here...unless Stone ratted me out. I take out my phone to call him, prepared to act like one of my soccer players throwing a fit over having to run laps. It rings one time as a door behind me opens.

I spin around, hoping to see Stella, though I know her apartment isn't 11H. A young African American woman about my age steps out with a friendly smile, looking me over. Almost like she knows who I am.

"Hi, are you looking for Stella?" she asks. Yep. She knows. My face must have twisted from confusion to horror, because she tells me her name is Hayden Bennett and that she is Stella's best friend. *No, Gracie Jameson is her best friend,* I think to myself. But then I remember I know nothing of her private life in New York. I only know her media persona and what little she's told me.

"Um, yes, ma'am, I am."

"Ugh, please. Don't call me ma'am. That's a Southern thing. I had to break Stella of the habit of saying it to every person we met who was older than us." She laughs in a reminiscing way. But then, in a more serious tone, she says, "You must be Lucas, the one making her absolutely senseless these days." I narrow my eyes, lifting a brow.

"What do you mean?"

"You're the man who had her glowing brighter than the Rockefeller tree while she was away. But you're also the man who has Stella in knots, not able to do her job because you are haunting her memories."

My face heats as the woman in front of me stares straight through to my soul as if she knows me. Like she knows Stella and me together.

"She was my fiancée," is all I manage to get out.

"I know, which is why I'm going to take you to her. I've never seen her so merry and bright, *pun-intended,* than she is with you. Her face when we FaceTimed...no woman has ever been more in love. And no woman has ever been more conflicted and distraught as she has been since she returned."

"She has?" I say, mouth open in disbelief. I saw the struggle in her eyes, the battle waging between being with me and her life here. But she chose here. Again.

"I don't know how you two are going to reconcile this, but I know she loves you. And you are here, which means you love her." Hayden's smile is one of promise. I think this woman has been talking to God about us because she seems to know everything. "Follow God's lead." Yep. God's talking to her. *Won't you just tell me, God?* I silently ask with a laugh.

"That's what I came for."

"Well then, Lucas Grady. Follow me and let's go get your woman before midnight strikes." I really, *really* like this Hayden Bennett person.

THIRTY-TWO

STELLA

M y mind constantly drifts back to campfires, cider, and Christmas in Dasher Valley. No matter how much I try to focus on New York City, on the buzzing crowd around me, on Bebe Rexha belting "In The Name of Love" on stage, nothing is keeping my mind occupied enough to not want to be somewhere quiet and cozied up with Lucas instead of freezing in my boots.

"She can sing. Who is this again?" Mama asks me. I don't miss that she is holding Brother Johnny's hand as he completely ignores everything around him except for Marian Harper. Who could ignore her or pass her by? Even with her illness, she is one of the most positive and radiant women that I know.

"Bebe Rexha," I say. Mama continues to bob her head to the music while drunk sorority girls and frat boys dance around us. I know a lot of people wish to be young again, but I don't. The only reason I'd want to be young again is to be with Lucas Grady once more. And man, I really wish his name, face, voice, and scent would fade away. Just for tonight.

It's nearing midnight. Only an hour away. I'm shocked Mama has made it this long. I thought for sure we would be back in the apartment sleeping by now. Well, they'd be sleeping, and I'd be having fitful dreams of Lucas. I've had the same dream over and over since leaving Mississippi. The same sugar-induced dream from a few weeks ago. And every time I wake up from it, the bliss from the dream is traded for a punch in the gut and a knife to the heart. He still hasn't called. Or texted. Radio silence. The type of silence that screams with how loud it is. He must have opened my gift by now. He must have read the letters and decided there is no future for us. Second chances do not happen the way all the romantic comedies claim they do. They are strictly for books and movies...not real life.

I understand. He doesn't want me to screw up his life again. I would be guarded against me too. I have no right to be upset with him, and I'm not. But I hate myself right now. Or at least I'm frustrated with stupid doesn't-know-what-she-truly-wants eighteen-year-old me.

No, I wouldn't want to go back to that age. I didn't know anything. I didn't know what true happiness was or how it was obtained. I didn't know what would truly fulfill me in life. I didn't know that my impact could be right where I grew up.

On another note, I decided what comes next for me. I've put in my applications, have been accepted, and now I wait out the New Year. Regardless of Lucas, I know what I want. I know what God is calling me to. So this next step in life is for me. Not for a man, not to rehash old flings, and not to escape. But to honor God's call and bring happiness back into my life.

Mama, Brother Johnny, and I cuddle close with blankets draped around us, watching our frozen breaths escape with every passing second. It's three minutes until midnight, and all I want is for Lucas to be here and kiss me as the ball drops and the clock strikes midnight. It glistens, sitting over 1 Times Square, waiting to bask in its glory, only to be put away as another year goes by. The clock continually ticks down, down, down until it reads 11:59:00pm. The buzz of energy in the air around us explodes like a dying star. And that's exactly how I feel, like an imploding star. Lonely, a million miles away from this moment.

Lucas is all I can think about. How his deep brown hair carries a slight curl. I picture his boyish smile and glistening gold eyes. I swear I can even smell his signature scent—sunshine and mint.

Everyone is counting down to the moment a new year begins. People all around me have made plans and resolutions, and they look forward to what the new year has to offer. I have to, though I'm nervous as all get out about my plans. *Let's just get this over with, please.*

10...9...8...7...6...5...4...3...

A hand grabs my shoulder, spinning me around until I am staring into familiar eyes that are brighter than the famous ball itself. Time stops, I'm sure of it. The counting fades out, the clock should be hitting 12 am by now. The crowd should be ringing in the new year.

But in this very moment, it's only Lucas Grady and Stella Harper. The moment belongs to us as if ordained by God. And by the smile on Lucas's face, it's the belated Christmas gift of a second chance.

The world roars back to life as "Auld Lang Syne" rings out across the sprawling city. Lucas wraps his arms around me, pulling me close to him. He closes his eyes, leans toward me, and places a gentle, warm kiss on my lips.

"Happy New Year," he whispers against my shocked, elated lips, his forehead resting against mine. The frigid night melts away as his warmth takes over.

This is home.

Home is not a state or a building or a career.

It's a person.

For me, it's Lucas Grady.

"Let's get out of here," I say, turning to Mama and Brother Johnny. I keep Lucas's hand firmly in mine as we turn to walk away. But then I run smack into Hayden.

"Hayden!" My screech gets lost in the noise of the crowd. She waves and smiles at me then joins our little posse. I lead the way with Lucas's arm looped through mine and Hayden's wrapped around my other one. Mama and Brother Johnny follow behind us. I barrel through the crowd, acting like a native New Yorker, until we make it to Four Five Coffee, which is staying open much later than usual for tonight's festivities.

We burst inside as the warmth envelops us. We look around at each other, and I love all the smiles going around tonight. Laughter bubbles out of me, and everyone else joins in. We laugh and laugh as the baristas look on, confused as to what is so funny. The reality? Nothing is funny per se, but everything is so, *so* right.

We eventually calm down and place our drink orders. During which the southern part of my cohort here is amazed at the variety of choices of milk, milk alternatives, and flavors.

"How do you like New York?" Lucas's face twists in horror at the question.

"I don't," he replies. "But I have to admit, there is a certain beauty to the cohesiveness of the city. Like a giant family."

"You can find family here." I nudge Hayden, who smiles and takes a sip of her coffee.

"I found this guy ringing your doorbell and decided to bring him to you," Hayden says, and I thank God that He brought me such an awesome friend—practically a sister—here in the city.

"Hayden is a phenomenal woman." Lucas echoes my thoughts. "At least from what I know of her so far." She shrugs him off and continues drinking her coffee. But I see the hint of a smile and the sparkle in her eyes that shows she is receptive to the character compliment. She practically raised herself, after all.

"Anyone who my daughter loves is a daughter of mine," Mama says, placing a disjointed hand on Hayden's shoulder. At that, Hayden's eyes water.

"Thank you, Mrs. Harper," Hayden whispers, holding back tears.

"Please, call me Marian. Why don't you take us back to Stella's apartment?" Mama asks Hayden. "Johnny and I are old people who need sleep."

"Let's go." Hayden bounds from her seat. "You two stay here and finish your coffee." She is off with a wink, and Mama and Brother Johnny follow behind. At the door, Mama turns around and says "bye" like Grandma Annie from *The Proposal* after giving the "baby maker" blanket to Margaret and Andrew. I roll my eyes and wave back and they disappear into the city.

"I read the letters," Lucas says after a moment. "That second chance thing? I want it. With you." His eyes hold mine and all traces of humor from the night are gone. "Come back to Mississippi with me."

My heart leaps and my stomach twirls. I already decided to go home, regardless of whether he would have me back or not. I have an application in to teach in the political science department at Southern Miss because I have a master's degree in political science. I made plans with Hayden to take over the campaign with me working from Mississippi until it's over, which I'm guessing she did not tell Lucas about on their journey to Times Square. But I had one more plan.

"Say something, Stella," Lucas pleads, his eyes full of worry.

"One condition."

"Anything." A smile tugs at his lips.

"I want my ring back." He reaches into the pocket of his jacket coat and pulls out a box. He opens it and sets a ring in the palm of his hand. My ring. From ten years ago. Tears flow down my face, my mascara going with it until it puddles up in drops on the table.

Lucas takes my left hand, slips the ring onto my ring finger, and kisses it. "I'm giving you my mother's wedding ring on our wedding day."

My heart leaps, and I give him my most genuine smile. "Thank you, Luca." I glance down at the ring on my finger. "I'm gluing this one on when we get home." He laughs, carefree and unabashed. *Home.*

"It's never coming off again." I stand up and he does the same. Leaning into his arms, I am complete. Home. Whole. Wanted. Loved. "You are my present and my future."

"Can't forget your past." He snickers. I tilt my head up, inviting his lips to mine.

Thank you, God, for Your plans.

EPILOGUE

HAYDEN, TWO MONTHS LATER

"You look stunning," I blubber to Stella as she twirls in her wedding dress. It is a simple white number with an open back and lace sleeves. It cinches at her waist, showcasing her curves flawlessly. "My bestie is so beautiful."

"Our bestie," Gracie Jameson, Stella's hometown best friend, comments with a grin from beside me. I hug her, already loving this bright southern flower. She is cute as pie, as they say down here in Dasher Valley, Mississippi, with her loose, bouncing blonde curls and blue eyes.

"You're right," I say.

"Do you think Lucas will cry?" Stella asks with a giggle, still swishing her wedding gown around.

"He'll try not to," Gracie begins, "but I don't think the man will hold it in. The big softy."

"Stella," her mom says as she enters the room, tears already pooling in her eyes. "My baby girl, you are so beautiful."

"Hmm, wonder where I get it from." She rushes to her mom and hugs her. The sinking feeling in my stomach that has been coming and going all day returns. I will never have this moment when...if...I get married one day. At least Stella has her mom to walk her down the aisle. I have no one.

"Okay, ladies," I pipe up, pushing my feelings deeper than a conspiracy theory hole. "It's time." Stella takes a deep breath as her mom, Gracie, and I exchange excited looks.

We usher Stella out of the dressing room, each taking a moment to make last-minute fixes to her hair and dress. We line up in the processional order with Lucas's groomsmen. My heart aches for a moment as I remember that Lucas's parents are deceased and not here to witness his wedding. Maybe that's why we connect so well? We're both parentless, not *that* old adults.

Though it's February, an instrumental version of "The Christmas Song" plays, signaling us to begin our walk down the aisle.

Gracie walks with Jared Helms, her fiancé, and I walk with Stone Harper, Stella's younger brother.

I don't miss the way his thumb slightly rubs against my arm as he escorts me down the aisle. Stella warned me he would try to hit on me. Much like he has done during every visit to New York.

We get to the end of the makeshift aisle in the back of Lucas's yard and break apart. Though it's a simple wedding, it's breathtaking. White chairs line both sides of the aisle hosting family and friends...and I think most of the little town. There is a wooden arch at the end decorated with dusty blue, white, and blush pink flowers and drapery.

Brother Johnny, who is engaged to Stella's mom, is officiating the union. So many engagements. My stomach sinks again as I reflect on my own singleness. It's self-induced because I am way too busy to entertain a man, but this is a wedding. Wishful thinking is a right of passage.

The wedding march begins, and Stella appears at the head of the aisle. Collective gasps, whispers, and sighs fill the air as the bride descends down the aisle. I take a swift glance at Lucas, who looks more than handsome in his black tux, and find a single tear rolling down his cheek. His awestruck smile fills me with a sense of hope, joy, and a twinge of sadness. I want a man to look at me like he is looking at my best friend right now.

But alas, it doesn't look to be in the cards for me.

Marian gives Stella's hand to Lucas before taking a seat in the front row. The look of pure bliss and undeniable love on their faces makes me a little weak in the knees. *Oh, I want that so very badly.*

I hear an echo of "Love Yourself" by Justin Bieber wafting ever so softly from Lucas's house. His backyard creates quite the acoustics. A few people notice and glance around, but everyone else seems to be too engrossed in the wedding. Stella and Lucas are highly engrossed in each other, for sure.

But I hear it, and I know it's my phone.

I also know it's Darcy Marshall, United States presidential candidate for the Independent Party, calling my phone.

Heat flares inside of me. Angry heat. He *knows* I'm at Stella's wedding and do *not* have time to deal with his pettiness. Ever since Stella transferred the campaign to me for the most part (she still does work from here in Mississippi), Darcy has been completely insufferable. More than he was in the beginning.

I push him out of my thoughts as the happy couple begins their vows. I paste a smile on my face and watch as they eventually seal the marriage with a very improper kiss.

I whoop and holler at their display of affection because Stella deserves this happiness.

They run down the aisle and we all follow before being whisked away for pictures, while the rest of the guests start transforming the backyard for the reception.

After the pictures, I run inside to get my phone. If I don't call the man back now, then I'll have double the dramatics from him later.

I pick up my phone, hit call back, and listen to the phone ring. He usually waits until the last possible moment to answer, so I'm utterly shocked when he answers on the third ring.

"Hayden," he answers, sounding out of breath. "I need your help." I roll my eyes. He probably needs someone to pick up his dry cleaning or something and the intern that usually does it is not available.

"I'm at Stella's wedding," I bite, but with the most respectful tone I can manage. He is running to be the president of the United States, after all.

"I know, and I'm sorry," he rushes. My body stills because Darcy Marshall has not once apologized to me for anything. "Priscilla broke off the engagement." A gasp escapes my lips unbidden.

"Wh—what?" I stutter. Priscilla is Darcy's girlfriend of two years and fiancée of only four months. I feel his panic and my hand rises to clutch my heart. There has only been one single president of the United States, and Darcy was not planning to be the second. The election is only nine months away.

"I don't know what to do, Hayden," he barks, "Tell me what to do. I am *not* losing this election because I am *wifeless.*" He continues to grumble under his breath.

"Breathe, Mr. Marshall," I say. I never call him Darcy to his face, or over the phone. "I'll be back in New York in two days, and we will figure something out. For now, I'll call our social media team to stay on top of the stories and make sure everything looks good and is in your favor."

"Just get here fast," he snaps before clicking off. I imagine his dirty blonde brows furrowed together as he paces, creating a trench through his office.

Shoot.

I'm going to have to find Darcy Marshall, the most prideful, insufferable man in existence, a wife in less than nine months. And make it look organic and natural.

How can a woman fall in love with Mr. Darcy?

If you enjoyed the story, please consider leaving a review on Amazon and Goodreads!

ALSO BY

DREW TAYLOR

Sign up for my newsletter where you will receive access to bonus scenes, additional chapters, extended epilogues, and much more! New content added at random!
Scan the QR code or click on the link to learn more about Drew Taylor's books!
www.drewtaylorwrites.com

ACKNOWLEDGEMENTS

Jesus, my Savior, to whom all glory and thanks belong. None of this would be possible without You. *Soli Deo Gloria.*

I never thought I would write a book. I had hoped, but always doubted. Yet here we are! Thank you so very much to every person who had a part in developing The Politics of Christmas. To my family—Mama, Dad, Turan, and Jace—you are my lifeline. Thank you. A special thank you to my besties (Kaitlyn, Aubrey, and Whitney) for being patient soundboards during this process and encouraging me every step of the way. To my church family (and Women of Faith group), who have prayed for me and over me through this season—THANK YOU.

Thank you to my developmental editor, Anne J. Hill, for kindly tearing the original story apart so that I could build it back so much stronger. Thanks to Callie, for the cute art on the cover! Lindsay Ranking, thank you for swooping in last minute for thorough proofread. A huge thanks to my beta readers who caught so many mistakes...it really does take a village! Thank you to my ARC readers for taking your time to read and review a little romance book from a new author. Special shoutout to L. Taylor (you know what you did!)

Thank you to #bookstagram. I found a community like no other with you lovely people. To all my online friends who have encouraged me heartily in the writing process (you know who you are) ...THANK YOU! I seriously do not think this book would exist without you. Finally, thank you to YOU, who just read this book of mine. A writer is nothing without her readers. Thanks for picking up a Christmas romance novel from a debut author and giving her a chance. You mean the absolute world to me.

ABOUT THE AUTHOR

Drew Taylor writes modern closed-door chick-lit romance stories from a Christian worldview. She believes faith-based romance can be full of heart, humor, healing, and hope while showcasing the reality of our fallen human condition. Her redemptive and engaging stories point to the One who embodies true love–Jesus Christ. Drew lives in the great state of Mississippi where she teaches high school English. When not teaching or writing, she enjoys reading, baking, researching conspiracy theories, and spending quality time with the people who mean the most to her.

Follow Drew:

Instagram: @authordrewtaylor

Facebook: Drew Taylor, Author

Pinterest: @authordrewtaylor

YouTube: @authordrewtaylor

Printed in Dunstable, United Kingdom